Eating the Fruit of Lies

A Novel

by Sandra Thompson Williams

ELM HILL

A Division of
HarperCollins Christian Publishing

www.elmhillbooks.com

D1441274

Eating the Fruit of Lies
A Novel

Published in Nashville, Tennessee, by Elm Hill, an imprint of Thomas Nelson. Elm Hill and Thomas Nelson are registered trademarks of HarperCollins Christian Publishing, Inc.

Elm Hill titles may be purchased in bulk for educational, business, fund-raising, or sales promotional use. For information, please e-mail SpecialMarkets@ThomasNelson.com.

Publisher's Note: This novel is a work of fiction. Names, characters, places, and incidents are either products of the author's imagination or used fictitiously. All characters are fictional, and any similarity to people living or dead is purely coincidental.

Library of Congress Cataloging-in-Publication Data

Library of Congress Control Number: 2019936366

ISBN 978-1-400325603 (Paperback)
ISBN 978-1-400325610 (eBook)

DEDICATION

Dedicated to all the couples who have been targeted by demonic forces. I pray that you will understand the importance of spiritual warfare as you take your place in prayer, the front line of every battle.

Special Thanks

Special thanks to my Lord and Savior Jesus Christ for trusting me to write and publish this novel. I also want to thank my family and friends for their encouragement.

CHAPTER ONE

"No, not me!" David yelled as he ran from the smoky confines of the room. He ran directly into the lightning and thunderous storm. He didn't look back just in case they were behind him. Panting and out of breath, he kept looking for a shelter. He felt like he had been running for miles.

"Where are all the people?" he mumbled to himself. "There's got to be somebody that can save me." No one was in sight. He kept running, although it was difficult with the heavy backpack he was carrying. In the distance he could see a fire, and shadows of small people seemed to be walking through it. He could hear the sound of horns blowing. The ominous clouds above him, even seemed to be shaped like horns. Everything was so weird. He saw some doors. He tried to open each within a matter of seconds. All were locked. He continued to run. There was no place to hide. Tears were streaming down, but he couldn't tell because the rain was blowing in his face. He was panicking. He was tired. The storm wasn't letting up.

The rain was turning into a hail storm. It appeared the next bolt of lightning would hit him. He used his arms to shield his face, as he began crouching to the ground. Somehow between sobs he yelled J-E-S-U-S and jumped straight up. He removed his sweaty hands from his face and opened his eyes. "Oh my God!" he said looking into the darkness of his bedroom. It was just another terrible nightmare. This time it was more real than the scary ones he had been dreaming. He reached across the night stand to turn on his little lamp. His Bible was on it. He grabbed it and sobbed, "Lord, please help me! I just don't know what to do!" He left the Bible on his bed, then got up to go to the restroom to wash his face. He was perspiring, in spite of the fact that it was only 68 degrees in his apartment. He liked it that way. Nice and cool. He wanted his whole life to be nice and cool. But for the last two weeks it had been anything but that.

His life at the age of 26 was being severely interrupted. He was having problems with his concentration at work, he had problems with his fiancé and he was generally just not himself. In fact, he didn't really have a fiancé anymore. He had called off the engagement that same week. He needed answers but he didn't know where to go.

Bending over the wash bowl, he watched the cold tap water go down the drain quickly. "My life is going down the drain too," he thought as he lifted his head and looked in the mirror at the bags under his eyes from lack of sleep. That was when he made up his mind to go and see the pastor. After all, he needed help. "If anyone can help me it should be the pastor," he thought.

He went back to bed and opened the soft leather cover of his Bible. The inside read, To David, my beloved son, in honor of your 21st birthday. It was hard to believe that five years had passed since his mother had given him the Bible. He quickly turned to the Psalms. He didn't want to start thinking about his mother, or his father for that matter. They've been separated now for two years. He was sure that any day now, they would start divorce proceedings. He was glad he was old enough to live on his own instead of having to choose between the two of them, like his sister had. It was no surprise to the family or anyone else that she chose to live with her mother. Now where is that passage? Oh yes, there it was, Psalm 4:8. The passage said he giveth his beloved peaceful sleep. He read it three times. Then he picked up his pen from the night stand and wrote down the dream. Next he adjusted his oversized pillow. There were only three remaining hours before his 6:00 a.m. alarm would sound off. He turned his light to the low setting and meditated until he fell asleep.

The next morning he was quite surprised at his alertness. When he left the shower, he went directly to the front door. He always read the morning paper before going to work. He felt it was his duty to know what was happening in the world. When he unlocked the two locks and opened the door, he nearly went into shock. There laying at his front door was a pleasant surprise. It was Sunday's paper in all its thickness carefully placed face up. "It's Sunday!" he exclaimed, realizing he had lost track of time. "What's wrong with me?" he thought as he stooped to pick up the paper and close his door. He decided to go back to bed because service wouldn't start for another three hours.

He took the paper, grabbed a banana from his kitchen counter and went back to bed. With the sunlight streaming through his vertical blinds he could make out an article at the bottom of the front page. CHRISTIAN MARRIAGES REACH 46% DIVORCE RATE!

He gasped. "Oh no," he said rubbing his head. Suddenly disgusted, he cast the paper on the floor and grabbed the remote control.

The morning news was on. He found an early morning news show and thought he'd hear something interesting, while deciding whether or not to get up. The lead story was about the divorce rate in America. "Fifty percent of first marriages end in divorce, 76 percent of second marriages end in divorce, 87 percent of third marriages end in divorce and 93% of fourth marriages end in divorce," rattled off some professor from a prestigious university. David quickly turned off the TV. His head dropped as he sat on his bed in bewilderment.

"Lord, just what are you trying to tell me?" he asked. Depressed and confused, he wondered why he cared so much about the Christian divorce rate. After all, he wasn't married. As a psychologist though, he counseled people day in and day out about their troubles, which very often included marriage. As a team member of the rather new Family Research and Counseling Center, he knew to stay detached from the people whom he counseled. When he was considering his career, he figured he could help more than the average psychologist because, as he always said to his friends, "I have a master's and I know the Master." "I've got to talk to my pastor today," he said out loud. "I've got to."

Service was not at all exciting to David on this Sunday. People around him seemed to beam with the joy of the Lord while he sat there like a rock in a storm. He could hardly wait for service to end so he could see the pastor. Dismissal finally came and he waited for the pastor to return to his office, after greeting everyone. David intentionally found a place where he could wait without having to talk to anyone.

A rather short and pudgy man is seated behind an old fashioned desk. The antique roll top was a gift from his rather prosperous congregation. The new carpet was quite complimentary. The very comfortable surroundings was one reason that he spent so much time in the office. After all, he had a very capable staff that could do everything from counsel to plan conferences. One chair that didn't quite match the desk was pulled alongside his desk. That was the chair that had been a favorite of his first wife. He didn't tell anybody his reason for keeping it. He just refused to let them dispose of it after her death. His desk was neater than he could ever keep it, thanks to the cleaning service that the church employed. He was rather proud of the fact that their church could employ members to do work for them. When he married again seven years ago, his new bride offered to clean his office, but he wouldn't hear of it.

"I have got to get the latest edition of the New Study Bible," he thought to himself as he took off his robe. He was hanging it in the office closet, when there was an unexpected knock at the office door.

"Come in," he said, as he wondered who was visiting him so soon after dismissal. David Edwards walked in with a strange look on his face. This young man who was barely twenty six was a faithful member of the church and his family had been members for two generations before him. But since his parents' separation, he was the only faithful member.

"Hello Pastor," he said while extending his hand for the customary greeting.

"Oh, hello Brother David," the pastor said as he shook his hand.

"That's right, I had forgotten that you asked to see me after service. Have a seat. I'm sure this must be about Rose."

David's mind wandered for just a minute as he thought to himself that the pastor must be angry with him. After all, he never called him Brother David in private. He was like a son to him. He focused his attention back on what the pastor was saying.

"She came in my room crying the other night and told me that you had called off the engagement. Now I don't usually meddle in my daughter's affairs, as you well know, but you were the one who told me you loved her and asked for her hand in marriage. Did you suddenly fall out of love?" he asked in his strong baritone preacher's voice.

"No sir," David answered in a nervous manner.

"So there isn't someone else?" Pastor Taylor asked, while returning to sit behind his desk.

"No sir!" David said emphatically, this time with his voice cracking. He wiped the perspiration from his forehead, and got up looking at the ceiling.

"Did something happen financially? Cause if you need a loan, I could —" Pastor Taylor was cut off by David in mid-sentence.

"No sir. That's not it," David said dropping his head. "I didn't really come to see you about Rose. Well not entirely. Although it does concern her."

"Then would you mind letting me in on what's going on? After all, you've been dating for a year," said this now irritated pastor and father who was groping for answers, information and whatever he could get from this person who seemed afraid to confide in him.

"Well, it's kind of hard to explain," David began.

"Try me," the Pastor quipped.

"Well," David began slowly, "it all began with a dream or maybe a nightmare," he said as he ran his fingers through his hair. "I'm still not sure which."

"Go on," said Pastor Taylor.

"Well, in my first dream, I was in the pit of hell listening to a conversation," David recalled with great difficulty. "Then after the conversation ended," he said speeding up the story, "I felt in my spirit that I couldn't get married until I had warned other couples about what I heard. So that's why I postponed our wedding," David said, feeling as if a load had been lifted from him.

"Well are you going to keep me in suspense or tell me about this dream?" asked Pastor Taylor as if he had been left hanging on a cliff with the rescuer watching. "Just slow down and start from the beginning," the pastor requested.

"Oh yes, sir. I certainly want you to know about it. You will have to help me warn the people. See, it- it all started two weeks ago," he stuttered nervously, "when I got on my knees to pray. You see I fell asleep, but it was a different kind of sleep. I seemed to be having a vision. There I was in the very pit of hell but no one saw me," David said in almost a whisper. "It was smelly and the, the awful eerie sounds of demons and smoke and horrible faces and, and"

"Well, go on son," said Pastor Taylor, "and speak a little louder."

David began to tell the story again as he relived this horrible experience.

"Satan and three demons are having a conference - you see," he began. "A banner reading Top Secret is hanging over what appears to be a chalkboard. I was hidden by smoke and the dimness of the room, but I could see him and hear his terrible deep and ugly voice. It was sickening," he said, holding his temples as if he had a headache.

"The demons were seated in classroom desks waiting for a meeting to begin. In walks Satan, holding papers.

"I'll make this brief," Satan tells the entire class. We don't have any time to waste. Then he calls out the name Deception."

Deception answers "Here."

Satan then calls for Discouragement, who also answers here. He keeps calling the names of demons who one by one answer to their name. He called for Destruction, Disillusionment, Division, Distraction, Disturbance and Debt.

Each demon answered "Here."

Then Satan tells them their new assignment. He hands out papers to them and tells them to look them over carefully. He brags to them that they have been very successful in their areas across Europe and in America. He tells them that the people on their lists have been singled out especially. He starts reading names from a list that seems to be endless. He turns on a slide projector.

Satan begins showing Victim 1 on a huge screen. It's a picture of a happy young lady in a bridal head piece.

Then he tells the demons that this is Darlene Smith. She's been married four years. She really expects to always be happy because she's a Christian. Satan says that he has assigned Deception to her. "Make your plans quickly," he says to Deception in a really deep voice. Destroy the marriage and the child!

Then he shows Victim #2 on a slide. It's a picture of a couple holding hands.

Satan's voice says, "This is Michael and Brenda McCain. They want children more than anything. I've assigned them to you, Discouragement."

Next Victim #3 is shown. Guess what? It's a picture of me. He tells them that I'm engaged to be married, then he says that he's got special destruction planned for me.

I sort of just cringed in the shadows. I didn't want them to see me, so I hid.

Then Satan says, "Deception what's your plan for Darlene Smith?"

Deception answers that he's going to build up a lot of confidence in her husband and then hit her with the truth of his unfaithfulness. Then he says that he's got the perfect person to tempt him into unfaithfulness and that their marriage will be irreparable.

All of a sudden there's a burst of applause from the demons. It was louder than a crowd cheering for an NFL touchdown.

Then Satan asks Discouragement, what does he have planned for the McCains. This demon was a hero. You could tell by the cheering, as he reported. He said he was going to use a classic case of dissatisfaction.

He said he'd play on their disappointment in not having children and build the case until they were both disappointed in each other. "It will be smooth," he bragged. Then he would work with Debt to turn them on each other.

Then Satan asks Destruction, "What's your plan for David Edwards?" As David tells this part of his dream, he begins to pace.

"I could only see them sort of whispering with excitement. Then Satan said, Wait a minute. This one we better keep confidential. I don't want any leaks getting out. It's close to the Saints 3:00 o'clock prayer time.

"I tried as hard as I could to hear, but I couldn't," David said with disappointment.

"All of a sudden, Satan raised his head and said, Oh, I couldn't have planned it much better myself. Alright team, there's one more thing. What area do we attack first?

The Demons simultaneously yelled, the prayer life! Then they dismissed themselves in a real disorderly way, after Satan had said report back to me in three weeks."

"After that, I sort of woke up," David said. "Even though I really was never asleep."

Pastor Taylor stood with awe just looking at David. "You mean, you're on Satan's hit list?" he asked in amazement.

"It appears so," said David. "But why me? Just when I was about to marry and enjoy a new part of my life. Now, I don't want you to get the impression that I'm afraid of the devil, cause I'm not. So don't think that. I suppose I should really be grateful that God is showing me the enemy's plan," he said with conviction. "I believe the Lord is leading me to consecrate myself and expose this devil. You wouldn't want me to marry your daughter under the current circumstances would you?"

Thunderous laughter roared from the pastor. David couldn't believe his eyes or his ears.

"You're overreacting," the pastor said between laughs. He actually wiped tears from his eyes.

David could feel the anger swelling inside of him or was it just embarrassment. He had confided in this man of God to no avail.

"You've just got the marriage jitters son," the pastor said matter-of-factly. "It's common to have second thoughts about the person you plan to spend the rest of your life with," he teased.

"Absolutely not!" David said in a very serious tone.

"Oh, the dream may be different, but that's all it is son. Just jitters. I tell you what," he said putting his arm around David's shoulder as he walked him to the door. "Just relax and take it slowly for a while. Your parents' separation is also weighing heavily on this situation. You'll see, everything will be back to normal in little or no time at all. You'll thank me for keeping you from making any rash decisions. You'll see."

"Let me ask you this," said the pastor. "Do you know any of these people that you saw at Satan's meeting?"

"Well no," answered David.

"Precisely!" said the pastor. "It's because they're not real," he said trying to convince the determined young man.

"But I saw faces!" said David, trying not to get too emotional.

"Oh, the mind has a way of constructing unreal images, especially when we're under stress," the pastor continued. "So be encouraged, young man. Everything will work out just fine."

With those words, he shut his office door and left David on the outside. David stood there stunned. "What is happening to me?" he thought. I'm tormented at home, and my own pastor thinks this is just pre-marital jitters. There was one thing that he knew. He knew he had to warn people, and with or without the help of the church leaders, he would accomplish this mission. He had other dreams he wanted to share, but now he knew that was impossible.

"God help me," he said, softly resisting the temptation to cry as he walked out of the church. "I don't know where to turn."

CHAPTER TWO

The dining hall was one noisy place for a Saturday afternoon. Everyone seemed to want to talk at once, while they drank tea and ate peanut butter cookies.

"Ladies, ladies," said Sister Marie as she gently tapped a glass with her spoon to get their attention. "First of all ladies, let me just say that I appreciate your coming here to share with each other this afternoon. Let's take our seats so we can get started. What we want to do is to just talk about our strengths and maybe we can help each other. Now just because I'm the pastor's wife, is no reason for you to think I can't relate to your problems. We're here to help each other and hopefully get answers from the Lord. After all, that's the purpose of the women's council group. Let's see, last week we talked about women supporting women," she said while looking over an agenda. "Today the subject is marriage. Let's start with the person married the least amount of time."

"Well, I guess that's me," said Sister Pearl; a smartly dressed business woman of twenty four.

"Tell everyone how long you've been married," said Sister Marie.

"Well, come next week," said Sister Pearl, "I'll have been married three hundred and sixty five thousand years." Laughter roared through the room. Everyone was broken up by the sudden humor of the newlywed who was approaching her first wedding anniversary.

"Sister Pearl, would you like to explain yourself?" asked Sister Marie looking puzzled.

"Sure," she answered as if she didn't know what the problem was. "The Bible says one day is as a thousand years and a thousand years is as one day. Next week completes my day of marriage," she said. "I didn't misquote the Bible, did I?" she asked, trying to keep a straight face. Everyone thought it was hilarious. Everyone except Sister Marie.

"We'll have to come back to you," said Sister Marie in a very serious tone. "Sister Marcie, you're a seasoned woman. What kind of advice can you offer these ladies?"

"Never go to bed angry ladies," said Sister Marcie.

"Now that's some sound advice," said Sister Marie, nodding her head approvingly.

"Find a way to cope with your anger. Re-channel it," continued Sister Marcie.

"What do you mean by that?" asked Sister Val who was normally too shy to ask questions.

"Well, I keep a list, a mental list that is, of who or what my husband reminds me of when I'm angry with him," said Sister Marcie. "For example, movie titles. When I'm angry, I add to the list. So far, these are the movies that remind me of him: *The Jerk, All Dogs Go to Heaven, The World, the Flesh and the Devil, Rosemary's Baby, Lady & the Tramp, Sleeping With the Enemy, Beauty and the...*"

"Sister MARCIE!" yelled Sister Marie, just in time to cut off the list. The whole room was again broken up with laughter. Sister Megan actually bit her tongue trying to eat a cookie and laugh at the same time.

"Ladies - what's going on here?" asked Sister Marie as she got up quickly. "This doesn't sound like a group of ladies where Christ is the center of the home. It's one more example of how the enemy has invaded the church." The mood in the room went from light-hearted to somber in a matter of seconds. "But let me tell you this, it's not the will of God for you to be husband-bashers or abused women. And I'm not talking about physical abuse," she said as she began to walk around the room. "Ladies,

I feel your pain," she said softly as the mood in the room caused many of the ladies to hold their heads down. She hugged Sister Marcie and said, "I know sometimes we hide behind laughter and smiles because we don't want people to see our hurt or our shame. We didn't call this meeting to embarrass anyone. I hand-picked you ladies today. I know you didn't know that. You thought all the ladies received invitations. Well, the Lord placed each of you on my heart and only you ladies know why."

Sister Pearl looked up at the First Lady. She now saw her in a different light. She saw Sister Marie Taylor as a lady of compassion.

"Can I say something Sister Marie?" asked Sister Pearl. "Sure honey," said Sister Marie; "but no more jokes."

"Well, that's just it," said Sister Pearl. "I know most of you know my husband, and you see a really great side of him. And, and I mean most of the time, he's really a nice guy," she stammered. "But, three days before our wedding, he called and said he needed to see me about an important issue that he couldn't discuss on the phone. Well when I met him that evening, he brought pre-nuptial papers with him. For some women, it wouldn't have been a big deal. For me it was devastating. I realized I was marrying someone who didn't completely trust me. I didn't know what to do. It seems his attorney buddies back at his office, advised him that this was a necessary step for his financial peace of mind."

"But he has never been married before, and he doesn't have children, does he?" asked Sister Val.

"No, it was our first marriage and neither of us had children," she said wiping a tear. "Well, the wedding was three days away. I gave him my best argument, but he said if I loved him I could see that this wasn't a big deal. I felt like I was between a rock and a hard place. I didn't want the embarrassment of canceling a wedding over something of this nature, so I signed it. It really hasn't been a big deal. Yet every time we have an argument, no matter how small, in the back of my mind, I always remember that pre-nuptial agreement and wonder how long before he will threaten me with it. I feel he has a bargaining chip to get things his way. And what do I have? I have nothing," she said in a pitiful manner.

Sister Marie moved toward Sister Pearl and gave her a big hug.

"I'd like to say something too," said Sister Marcie, in a rather low voice. "I was told that the honeymoon would last for at least a year, but we found ourselves fighting after three weeks." We would argue over anything. Finally I would just let him have his way. So far, our marriage has lasted six years. The funny thing about it is that I think he's happy. After all, he gets his way in just about everything. All the reasons, that I got married seemed to go down the proverbial toilet. I wanted someone who would stand up for me and be a true companion, yet my husband craves all the attention. Perhaps, it's because he is an only child. I just don't know anymore." Tears rolled down her eyes.

"Ladies, I've even found myself praying to God that one day I would wake up and find out that I had been in a coma for the last few years. I just wanted to start over and wipe the slate clean. But I know that I can't go backward, so I hide, many times behind humor," she said looking over the room at her good friend Val.

"Well, since confession is good for the soul," said Sister Val, "I might as well confess that my marriage wasn't made in heaven either. We seemed to start off ok, but then I noticed that many of our friends seemed to know things that were going on in our house. I don't mean what we had for dinner, but they'd know about our arguments, they'd know when and where we made up. They'd know what we discussed in bed. It got to a point that nothing was sacred. He seemed to always deny telling his friends things about us. But I don't talk to anyone about private matters. If I'm not important enough to be sacred in his life, what is?" she said to the group.

"You're right Sister Val," said Sister Marie. "We've believed every Cinderella story we've seen, then when something happens to us, we go into shock. It's hard to admit we've made a mistake in marrying the wrong person," she said.

"I didn't really plan to speak up," said Faye Edwards, probably the most attractive woman of her age group among them. "Please don't fall into the trap, where I fell. I had a decent husband, he wasn't perfect, but who is? He was a hard worker and a good father, but somehow we drifted apart. Nothing I did was good enough anymore. I'm not sure how I became that way, but I gradually was someone that he hated and I didn't care anymore. He opted out. Now we're both two lonely people. I keep telling myself that I'm better off, but am I? I feel it was my fault because I didn't seek God during the trouble. Instead, I read magazines and listened to talk shows. One thing I am sure of, I'm going on with my life."

"Yes," agreed Sister Marie. "We are all going on in Jesus' name. I feel the spirit of Disappointment in the room. Can we pray, right now and cast this demon out?"

The women all seemed to agree as they gathered close together.

"Ladies, let's join hands," said Sister Marie. The entire group began to pray.

Chapter Three

The smells of hell and the shrieking sounds are enough to give you a double migraine and put your teeth on edge, David thought. Apparently, a meeting is going on, he assumed.

"Look Discouragement, I sent you to do a job, but you botched it up," Satan said to the demon.

"I can't help it if the plan backfired. Some spirit-filled woman sensed I was there and cast me out," he said expecting sympathy.

"I don't want any excuses," said Satan in a threatening way.

"Don't let it happen again. If you can't ruin a simple ladies fellowship, I can't depend on you to ruin relationships and marriages. Now get your act together and get out," he shouted in a horribly deep voice.

"Mr. Edwards, Mr. Edwards, Mr. Edwards," yelled the division secretary. David jumped up from his desk and almost stood at attention. "Yes, Miss Walker?" he answered. "Oh, I've been calling your phone, but you didn't answer. So when I knocked and you didn't answer, I wanted to make sure you were ok."

"Yes, I'm fine," he said rubbing his eyes." "I must have dozed off for a minute," he said.

"Well your next client is here," said Miss Walker. "Should I show her in?"

"Sure," he said. "Just give me a moment to review her file."

What's going on with me? David thought. One minute, I'm having clients and the next minute I've gone to hell and back.

"I think this is going to be a long day," he said. He grabbed his schedule and focused on his afternoon appointments.

A quick peruse of the file reminded him that his next client was new to counseling. There wasn't much there on the form each person was required to fill out before consultation. But there was one thing there that left him stunned. Her name was Darlene Smith.

There were two knocks at the door and a young lady entered. She was quite attractive and didn't appear to be more than twenty five. Her warm smile added an aura of confidence in the way she carried herself. She appeared friendly, yet reserved. The truth, if it were to be told from her face, was hidden in her eyes. Somehow for a person of her distinction, they should have been gleaming. Instead they were dull and showed signs of past hurt.

"Good afternoon," she said as she shut the door behind her.

"David Edwards," he said extending his hand for a shake and gesturing for her to be seated. "How are you today Ms. Smith?"

"Well, I think physically I'm fine," she said. "But please, call me Darlene," she insisted.

"But I like the name Smith," David said. "It's such an unusual name."

She threw her head back with a delightful laugh. "Thanks for making my nervousness go away," she said.

"How long has it been since you've laughed?" he asked, sensing the Spirit of Disillusionment.

"Too long," she said staring at the furnishings of the office.

"Well, I hope we can change that for you. Can you tell me a little bit about yourself?" he asked, while reaching for his notepad and pen.

"Well," she said looking up as if the answers would come from the ceiling, "I'm twenty four. I completed college two years ago with a degree in liberal arts. I work for a publishing company downtown and I like to swim and shop."

"Wow," said David. "That certainly was concise. Almost as if you had rehearsed it."

Darlene turned her eyes toward the window and said nothing.

"Who recommended you come to see us for a consultation?" he asked.

"My job," she said.

"Do you know why they did that?" he asked, once he had gotten her attention again.

"They said I showed signs of depression," she answered.

"I see," David said. "Tell me, have you had a weight loss within the last few months?"

"Yes," Darlene answered. "I lost about twelve pounds. But I really wanted to lose weight," she said, trying to sound convincing.

David made a few notes on his paper before asking more questions. "Do you attend church?" he asked.

"Yes, I love attending church. I'm very faithful to my local assembly and I'm quite involved in church activities!" she said with the most enthusiasm she had mustered since walking into the office.

Staring directly into her eyes, he went on with his next question. "Darlene, are you happy?"

She lowered her head and reached for her purse. She had barely retrieved two white tissues from the compact holder before the tears began to flow.

After sobbing uncontrollably for a good three minutes, she opened up to David. She talked about her marriage, her 14 month old child and her suspicions of another woman. David just sat there and listened. He could not tell her that he had seen her situation in a vision. She might not believe him. He wasn't quite sure of the next step.

"Well, I think my 30 minutes are up," Darlene said. "I've got to get back to work. I really do feel better. Somehow I believe confiding in you has helped me. This is very unusual, cause I never talk to strangers about myself," she admitted.

"Believe me, everything you've shared will be kept in the strictest confidence," he said.

She got up to leave and he walked her to the door.

"Everything is going to be alright," he said. She shook his hand, smiled and walked away.

After closing the door behind him, David let out a deep sigh of relief. A small piece of the puzzle had come together. But what was next?

Chapter Four

The phone was ringing off the hook when he arrived at his apartment. He let the machine answer it. It was Rose.

"Hi David, please call me when you get in. I need to know if you're going to Shady Tree Nursing Center to visit Aunt Tillie with me. The last time we went together you promised her you'd come back this month. Please call me and let me know. Thanks. ....Goodbye."

There was a slight hesitation before she said goodbye.

He wasn't quite sure what he should do. He didn't want Rose to get any ideas that the marriage was back on, but he didn't want to hurt sweet Aunt Tillie. Although she wasn't his real aunt or Rose's for that matter, he seemed very close to her and a promise was a promise.

Aunt Tillie had been very kind to him when his parents broke up. She'd call him and console him as if he were her own child. When in fact, she had no children of her own. After she fell and broke her hip, there was no choice except for her to go into the nursing home so she could be looked after properly. She considered the move temporary. Although she was 78 years old, her mind was really quite sharp. She was always considered a prayerful woman by the entire congregation.

He picked up the phone and dialed Rose's number. "Hi, I got your message about Aunt Tillie. If you can be ready in two hours, I'll pick you up."

"Sorry, David," she said. "I can't go, but please don't let that stop you.

My father just asked me to type some information for him that he needs right away."

"Well, I'm sorry you can't go," said David. "But I think I'm going to go anyway, just to let her know I haven't forgotten my promise."

"I'm sure she'll appreciate that," said Rose.

"Well take care of yourself," David said after a short pause.

"I'm doing the best I can," she said in a rather sad way. "Goodbye."

"Bye now," he said feeling rather strange. This was the first time they had spoken since the breakup. At least she wasn't crying, he thought.

The drive to the nursing home took the better part of 35 minutes. It was an interesting ride as David pondered over and over what he would say to Aunt Tillie about his breakup. He didn't want to hurt her. She was quite happy when he told her of his engagement.

He pulled into the parking lot and noticed a sign on the door of the building. "Residents are being evaluated today. Visitors welcome after six."

It was 5:45 p.m. David resolved to wait in the receiving room.

"Hi, I'm here to see Miss Tillie Green," he said to the receptionist.

"Would you please bring her to the visiting room at 6:00 p.m.?"

"Yes, your name sir?" she asked kindly.

"David Edwards," he replied as he took his seat. He picked up a magazine, yawned twice and fell somewhere between a trance and asleep. He caught himself as he began falling out of his chair. The sudden jerk of his head brought him back to reality. When he opened his eyes Aunt Tillie was being wheeled into the room.

"Davie, sweetie," she said in the most loving voice. "Come and give Auntie some sugar," she said.

David immediately jumped up and went to hug and kiss her. "It's been so long since I've seen you," she said. "I thought you forgot about this little old lady," she teased.

"Oh, I could never forget you, Aunt Tillie," he smiled. "Never in a million years."

"How've you been, dear?" she asked in a loving way. "Are you treating yourself right? How are you coming with those wedding plans?"

His expression totally changed as he stood up straighter and put one hand in his pocket.

"Wedding plans are sort of on hold for now Aunt Tillie," he said cautiously.

"Well that explains my dream," she said. He turned and looked at her straight in the face.

"You're not shocked?" he asked.

"Oh honey, I was praying for you last week, when I had a dream that indicated you were not quite ready for marriage."

"Well, what was it about Aunt Tillie?" he asked.

"Oh it wasn't much to it son," she said.

"Please tell me Aunt Tillie," he begged.

"Well, she said, adjusting her false teeth with strange mouth movements. "I saw your darling little fiancé standing at the altar. She kept motioning for you to come to her. You were in the back of the sanctuary. Then I saw you from behind. You reached in your pocket and brought out a pocket watch. You opened it, shook your head and put it back. Then you appeared to be walking in the opposite direction of the altar."

"Wow," said David. "Do you think I left because it wasn't the right time?" he asked in a rhetorical way. "Did you tell anyone about this dream Aunt Tillie?" he asked.

"Oh no honey, it wasn't the sort of thing that I'd tell people who aren't involved," she said.

"Do you dream often Aunt Tillie?" he asked in a very serious tone.

"When I was your age, my family called me the Dreamer," she said with a laugh.

David pulled a chair close to hers and sat down. "Do you enjoy your dreams?" he asked.

"Truthfully, David," she said, "I wish I would never dream. It's one of those gifts from God that you can't explain. When I was first united to our church, I made the mistake of sharing some dreams with members of the congregation that I didn't know very well," she said. "It turned out to be a bad idea. A rumor was started that I was a psychic and people responded by treating me unfairly. They either told me every single dream they had, hoping for solutions to their problems, or they steered clear of me as if I was a witch."

"How terrible," David said in a sympathetic way. "I have something I would like to share with you, but I need to pray about it first," he said.

"That's fine honey," she said. "It's always good to consult the Lord about everything," she continued.

The ride home was much quicker than the ride to the nursing home. David wanted to actually meditate before the Lord concerning his dilemma. Should he or shouldn't he tell Aunt Tillie about his dreams? The pastor didn't believe him. Would she? What about the proof of Darlene Smith? That was certainly no coincidence.

He was nearly home now. The first thing he planned to do was to look for his reference Bible. There was something in there about dealing with dreams that he wanted to investigate.

CHAPTER FIVE

Darlene lifted little Janie and put her into the playpen. She was passing a rattle to her when the door knob turned and her husband appeared.

"Hi Keith," she said, trying not to sound too happy to see him. She actually was very happy to see him. He was actually home on time, which meant he came straight home, and perhaps was happy to see her as well. But just in case he wasn't, she lowered her eyes and put her attention back on Janie.

He approached her and kissed her on the forehead. She wished he hadn't done that. It was a cold kiss. She could have gotten more passion from her dog.

He sat in the big easy chair that they both used to snuggle in together. He put his head back and just closed his eyes.

"Is everything alright?" she asked him sincerely.

"What do you mean by that?" he answered.

"My mother always said never answer a question with a question," she replied. He continued to stare at her.

"I just meant that you looked tired; maybe you had a rough day," she continued.

"Oh sure," he said. "Yes, I am a little tired and yes today was kind of a rough day in the office."

"Want to hold Janie?" she asked.

"Actually I'm a little sleepy," he said. "I think I'll lie down for a while. Just wake me when dinner's ready."

She didn't respond. She just waited until he had closed the bedroom door before letting the tears fall. She could take it if he was upset with her, she thought, but he shouldn't ignore our baby.

The infant tried to catch the tears as they fell. Perhaps sensing her mother's unhappiness or just out of instinct, she threw her arms around her mommy's neck and said something completely in babble.

"I love you too," Darlene said, hugging baby Janie as tight as she dared. She then kissed her cheek and left her with her toys.

Darlene got up and went into the kitchen to prepare dinner. The phone rang as she headed toward the refrigerator. She thought Keith might get it; he didn't. It stopped after three rings. He suddenly came out of the bedroom.

"Who was the call for?" he asked.

"I don't know, it stopped after the third ring," she said. "Maybe they realized it was a wrong number," she continued.

"Yea, maybe so," he said. "What's for dinner? I have a taste for shrimp."

"Well, I was planning on making a casse-"

"Another casserole?" he asked. "Not for me," he said. "I think I'll get some shrimp at Rene's Café. I know you don't like their shrimp, so go on with the casserole," he insisted.

Twenty seconds later he was out of the door and she heard his car engine give that usual revving sound as he took off down the street. She was quite stunned by the suddenness of his departure. She kept rehearsing in her mind everything that happened. First he said he was tired. Then he said he was sleepy. Minutes later he wants shrimp and he leaves in an awful big hurry. She then remembered the telephone ringing and coming to an abrupt stop.

Oh God! she thought to herself, was that a signal? She suddenly lost her appetite. She was recalling every suspicious move he had made lately. She didn't want to believe he was seeing someone else. But every time she was convinced that he might be unfaithful, she told herself she was overreacting. Consequently, she would lose her appetite and her nerve for confronting him about her suspicions.

She decided then to go and see the counselor again. Maybe he could offer her some advice. She felt she could use some at this point in her life. She wasn't sure how much more uncertainty she could live with.

"Lord, don't let me be a fool," she said aloud. "I just don't want to be anybody's fool."

CHAPTER SIX

David thumbed through the concordance many times before he ended up with three passages. He read about Joseph's dreams, Daniel's dream and Peter's dream.

It appeared to him that those who God dealt with in dreams had revelations or warnings for the present or future. From what David could really understand, Joseph revealed his dreams too early and it got him into trouble with his brothers. Daniel's dream is still being interpreted today because it has yet to be fulfilled. Peter's dream was to be shared with others right away because it had a purpose to help people in their present situation. David felt that he was in this category. His dreams must have to do with the present, otherwise God never would have sent Darlene into his office. His mission must be for the present. He needed to warn people about Satan's plans.

David felt somewhat relieved. Now the question was whether or not Aunt Tillie could help him. She certainly was prudent enough. She's had previous experiences with God and dreams, he reasoned to himself. He was pacing the floor by now and weighing pros and cons. She already knew about the breakup between Rose and me, he thought. He was start-ing to feel exhausted. He sat down on the couch and quickly fell asleep.

The blackboard read Phase II. All eyes were focused on someone giv-ing a report. David identified him, because he had seen him before. It was Deception. "In my conclusion," Deception said, as if giving a motivational speech, "remember to hit them quickly like a ton of bricks. Don't give them time to regroup before coming at them again and again. It almost always works. They'll be too dazed and upset to remember who to call on, if you do it right."

"Enough of that," a voice shouted from out of nowhere it seemed. "What's your next step?" asked Satan.

"Well I've got her scared and suspicious and next I'll plant the divorce option so that she considers getting one everywhere she turns," the demon explained. Then he broke into a sick laughter. "She doesn't know that he hasn't really committed adultery yet," he laughed. The entire room was broken up in a laughter. David was stunned as he witnessed this. Then he heard a bell ring. It was ringing over his head and he was horrified. He didn't want them to see him. Although he couldn't see it, he reached up and grabbed the bell to silence it.

"Hello, hello, David?" a voice said. David sat up straight. He was startled to find the phone's receiver in his hand. He shook himself as in disbelief. The bell was the ringing of the telephone. He put his mouth to the receiver and responded with a hello.

"Hi honey," a voice said. "It's Mom. Were you asleep?" she asked.

"Oh, hi Mom," David answered. "I was just napping. I haven't heard from you in a week."

"Did you forget that I was out of town?" she teased.

"Oh, that's right," he said. "I really missed you," he told her with sincerity.

"I missed you too, baby," she said. "Although when I am in town, you don't visit me like you should," she briefly scolded.

"I'll have to do better," he explained. "I've just been a little preoccupied lately."

"Have you seen your father lately?" she asked.

"Not for about a week," he answered.

"Then he hasn't talked to you about Rose?" she asked.

"What do you mean?" he questioned.

"Oh, your father called me while I was out of town and left a message on my voice mail. He said he saw Rose by chance the other day and she told him the wedding plans were called off. Is that true?"

"I'm sorry Mom. I had planned to tell you both, but there were some things I needed to work out first," he explained.

"Well, if you want to discuss it honey, I'm here for you. I wish someone had counseled me before I married your father. Maybe things would have turned out differently. Your father said Rose looked, well, terrible; like she'd been crying a lot. I don't know what she did, but it must have been pretty awful for you to break your engagement. But trust me, it's better that it happened now than after you were married," she said.

David just held the phone while she talked. He kept wondering to himself if everyone else was blaming Rose too. That wasn't fair to her.

"Mom," David said, interrupting her constant talking. "One day I'll go over everything with you, but I really need to take care of something right away," he explained.

"Alright, baby, just remember I'm here for you," she emphasized.

"Talk to you later," he said as he put the receiver down. He stood up and walked toward his picture window. He could only make out shadowy images on the outside. His heart was aching. The young woman whom he still loved dearly was unjustly being blamed for their breaking up. He knew he had to fix that situation. She deserved so much better. Yet without an explanation, he had called off their engagement. He walked back over to the phone and sat down to call her. Would she want to discuss this with him? He would try to make her understand. He could feel his heart beating faster as the phone rang. A soft voice answered.

"Hello Rose," he stammered. "This is David and I'd like to talk to you."

"About what?" she asked in a rather neutral tone. "I feel like I owe you a better explanation than what I gave you earlier."

"You aren't feeling guilty are you?" she asked curtly.

"Would you just give me about 10 minutes of your time?" he pleaded.

"Alright," she said, giving in; although she kept her feelings guarded.

"I'm coming to pick you up, say in about twenty minutes," he said.

"I'll be ready," she replied with a little hesitation.

The drive to Rose's house was one of both apprehension and excitement. The evening seemed especially fresh as he drove with the windows lowered, just enough to taste the freshness of the air. He was only a few blocks away when he heard a faint ringing. He was puzzled for a moment until he realized it was his cellular phone. He could hardly hear it because it was inside his brief case. He slowed down at the yellow light and waited for it to turn red. No one was behind him in this city of 70,000 people. He reached into the backseat with his long arms and got the brief case. He opened it just in time for the changing of the light. Maybe Rose is calling to see how far away I am," he thought. It was rather unusual for someone to call him on his cellular phone during the evening hours. "Hello," he answered, with curiosity in his voice, "this is David."

"David," said a frantic voice on the other end. "I need you baby!" He was rather stunned to hear her tone of voice.

"Mom?" he said in bewilderment. "What's wrong?" he asked, as he pulled the car out of traffic into a parking lane. "It's your sister," she said. "She's unconscious, and I can't wake her up," she said nearly whispering while trying to hold back the tears.

"Mom call 911," he instructed. "Don't panic, I'll be there as soon as I can." After checking in his rear view mirror, he made a U-turn and began the twelve minute trip across town to his mother's house. "Lord, please let her be alright," he prayed aloud. She's got to be alright, he thought. For as long as he could remember, he'd taken care of his little sister, watching out for her, giving her advice, lending her money. Only during the last year had he noticed a change. It was definitely the result of the separation. She seemed to have moved into her own private world. She'd call him on the phone, but their level of confiding was somehow different. Then she started some ridiculous diet, he remembered, that was totally unnecessary for a girl of 5 foot 5. She was actually pretty and had what he considered an ideal weight. He wondered if she was still on the "fad" diet pills that he had scolded her for taking more than three months ago.

David tried to clear his mind of negative thoughts, in order to pray for his sister. She needed help now and scolding was not going to help.

When he pulled into the driveway, he had to maneuver around the ambulance. That's when he noticed his father's Chevy. He felt a little better, but was afraid to be too optimistic until he could see his sister. He entered through the side door that was so familiar to him as a child.

He walked through the kitchen and headed down the hall toward the bedrooms. The pictures that told the story of his family for most of his childhood were no longer lining the wall of the paneled hallway. They had been replaced with modern art. It was a painful walk. But today wasn't the day to deal with his pain, there were matters of greater importance. He heard voices coming from his sister's room.

Two paramedics were attending to her. One was a rather muscular young man who David thought couldn't have been much older than he was. He was completing a blood pressure procedure. The other attendant was a woman about 45 years old who was asking questions. His sister's eyes widened as David came through the door. "I'm alright," she said, extending her right hand for him to hold. David sat on the paisley designed bedspread that was folded back on her daybed. He sat on the side opposite the paramedics and looked to them for information. "This is my brother David," said Stephanie smiling. Her eyes looked weak from exhaustion. Her brother noticed that her color was unusually faint and the only thing around her glowing was the bright lamp on her night stand. In one glance he could see that her room had changed a lot. She once had her walls covered with plaques of honor and certificates of recognition. Now they were nowhere in sight. This could have been anybody's room. It was certainly not one where pride was evident. Yet it was clean. With a quick sweep of his eyes around the nicely furnished room, he felt he was in a sterile environment like an institution.

"Hi Steph," he said. He ignored her hand and hugged her while sitting on the edge of her bed. "Are you OK?" he asked in a voice of compassion.

"That's what we're trying to find out," answered the female paramedic. "One thing's for sure," she continued, "we recommend that she cease taking these diet pills and discard them immediately. My daughter once took that stuff," she said, shaking her head in disbelief. "I don't know how the FDA ever allowed it on the market," she continued. "I also think she should come in for a thorough examination."

"I don't want to go," said Stephanie looking at David for support.

"Where's Mom and Dad?" he asked.

"They're in Mom's bedroom discussing me," she said.

"I'll be right back after I talk to them," said David. He hurried down the carpeted hall and stood in the doorway. It was obvious that they didn't hear him coming or see him standing there because they kept talking. His Mom was sitting on her bed wiping tears while his Dad was turned with his back toward the door.

"I didn't say it was your fault," his Dad snapped. "I just said you should have known about her diet pills. After all, she does live with you. You might as well stop crying. It's not going to help the situation. If we don't send her to the hospital, you'll have to watch her closely the next few days to make sure she's alright." His father reached into his pocket and handed a handkerchief to her. She lifted her head and extended her hand. That's when she saw David.

"Hi baby," she said, quickly fixing her face to smile. His father turned and said, "Hey, guy, when did you get here?" while he patted him on the shoulder.

"I've been here a few moments," he said. "What's the deal with Steph?" His parents looked at each other and then back at David. His father spoke first. "Well, your mother seems to think the diet pills caused a bad reaction."

"That's not what I said at all," she responded, getting up from the bed. "I said she's been taking them longer than she should have been and her body doesn't need them and..."

"But a moment ago," her father interrupted, "you said that-"

"Dad, it really doesn't matter," David said cutting him off. "What are we going to do now?" he asked.

The drive back home was rather disturbing. David wasn't quite sure why. He was glad Stephanie was feeling better. She walked him to the door before he left. He made her promise to call him the next day to make sure there were no side effects. His father left before he did. His face showed signs of anger or was it guilt? It was eleven o'clock when David left. He had a very uneasy feeling. He came to a rather sudden stop at the traffic light when he remembered Rose. He couldn't believe it. After he got the call from his Mom, visiting Rose completely slipped his mind. He pounded the steering wheel with his fists. He was completely angry with himself. How could she ever trust me again? he thought. I've disappointed her at least twice.

"Lord, what is it with me?" he said aloud. He pulled his car over and got his phone out of his briefcase again. He had placed it there at his Mom's house, because he didn't think he would need it. He convinced himself to call her in spite of the time. David got out of the car and leaned against it as he dialed her number. "Hello," a sleepy voice answered after five rings. For a moment, he thought he had the wrong number, probably because he expected and wanted Rose to answer so badly. "Hello," said David. "May I please speak to Rose?" he asked nervously.

"Hello David, this is Sister Marie."

"I, I apologize for calling so late Sister Marie, but I had an emergency this evening," he explained. "Are you alright David? You weren't in an accident were you? Rose was pretty worried about you. She said you should have been here hours ago," said Sister Marie in a voice that was both concerned and scolding at the same time. "Rose finally went to bed. She was rather angry, I don't mind telling you."

"It's my fault," David admitted. "I know she probably won't speak to me, but I really was only a few minutes from your house when my Mom called to tell me something had happened to Steph," he explained.

"Is she alright?" exclaimed Sister Marie.

"Well the paramedics believe her diet pills gave her a bad reaction. Mom couldn't wake her up for the longest time. "But she's fine now."

"Why on earth is Steph taking diet pills?" she said bluntly, sounding more like the pastor's wife he was accustomed to hearing. "Why that young lady's already thin as a rail. But then again," she said more calmly, "separations and divorces cause unusual reactions from children. But I don't need to tell you that," she said. "What do you mean by that?" he asked defensively.

"Oh David, just look at you," she said. "Sunday you looked as if you hadn't slept in God only knows how long and ..."

"My breaking off the engagement, Sister Marie, had nothing to do with my parents' separation," he interrupted. "Actually," he said, starting to walk down the street, "I think I handled it as well as anyone could. And I don't want people blaming my folks for my broken engagement," he almost yelled. "It was not cold feet and it wasn't Rose's fault and..."

"David calm down," said Sister Marie in a concerned tone. "You're getting yourself worked up over nothing," she said.

"Well it may be nothing to you, but to me it's really serious," he said. "No one seems to quite understand what I'm going through or rather dealing with," he said walking faster, "I just..."

"David," interrupted Sister Marie, "it's been a long day and we're both tired," she said trying to bring closure to their conversation. "Why don't you try to contact Rose later. She's a pretty reasonable girl," she said.

"Do you think she'd listen?" he asked more humbly. "I really am sorry," he said in a softer voice that nearly broke up.

"I believe you are," answered Sister Marie. "But I can't fix things between you and Rose, I will tell her that you phoned and that Steph is doing better," she said.

"I'd really appreciate it Sister Marie," he said. "And would you pray for me?"

"David," she said lovingly, "I know I'm not your mother or Rose's real mother if the truth be told, but you both are always in my prayers," she said.

When they had said their goodbyes and hung up, David realized he had walked nearly a block from his car. He had ended up directly in front of the Salvation Army. He was surprised to find that he had walked so far. The building was under renovation. Seeing it reminded him of the article he had read recently featuring the building in last week's paper. The building was more than 80 years old. It was under Phase I of the renovation, the ripping out stage. There was ragged carpeting laying on the sidewalk awaiting the trash collectors to haul it off. There was also something shiny beneath the carpet that caught his eye. One corner was hanging out just enough to light the darkened area whenever a car's headlight hit it. His curiosity moved him to lift the carpet, which was discarded in a very large roll to lie flat on the sidewalk near the curve probably to be hauled away before morning. David wondered why they hadn't rented a dumpster for the material, as he stooped to touch the glimmering part of the object. He ran his fingers along the shape of this strange object which appeared to be a horn of some type. It was a little larger than his hand and covered in a gold color. He managed to pull the object from beneath the rubbish and discovered another matching horn on the other side of the plank of wood that was between it. It looked as though this was a mantle for a fancy fireplace. Yet, on second thought, David reasoned that it was probably placed on top of a table that belonged at the altar of the chapel. It looked more like a replica of the Ark of the Covenant.

He wondered why they were getting rid of it. Not that it was of any real value, but it had an antique design to it. He knew he had inherited a knack of collecting odds and ends from his father. When he was younger his father would take him to garage sales, estate sales and cheap auctions. He used to hate going, but he found himself one day following in the footsteps of his father. He would stop at garage sales to make sure there were no bargains calling him by name. His father had a weakness for old tools and unusual items. Sometimes he would clean them up and resell them.

David lifted the table top from the heap of trash and began carrying it toward his car. Surprisingly, it was kind of heavy. He held it away from his clothes just in case there were splinters on the wood. What a night it had been. He wondered if he should be feeling guilty for acquiring such a find. Perhaps this is God's way of letting me know all is not lost, he thought to himself. After all, if he hadn't gone to see his sister, he wouldn't have come down this street. If he hadn't remembered that he had forgotten to call Rose, he wouldn't have parked his car. If he hadn't been angry and upset, he wouldn't have walked down to the Salvation Army building.

"This must be an omen," he thought. As he opened the trunk of his car, he said in nearly a whisper, "All things work together for good to those who love the Lord and are the called according to his purpose." He adjusted the table top with horns, several times before it fit into the trunk of his car. As he drove home, he wondered where he would put it. He didn't have a fireplace. But he did have the coffee table given to him by his mother. He kept it in the guest bedroom that he used as an office. It was too small to ever let anyone sleep in there. He used it to iron his clothes and work on his computer. Sometimes he evaluated clients and documented the information at home on computer. He would try that when he reached home. He was glad to have something else to think about other than his problematic relationship with Rose. "I hope I'm able to rest tonight," he thought. "I just want to rest."

CHAPTER SEVEN

When morning came, the sun seemed to tap David on the shoulder as blades of light peeked through the crevices of his bedroom blinds. He sat up in bed and looked around him as if in a strange place. Something was different. What was it? After a moment he realized what it was. He had slept completely through the night. Not once had he visited the pits of hell. He smiled, rested his head on his pillow and said, "Thank you Lord."

The office was filled with clients when he arrived. They sat in the waiting area, anticipating being called by one of the three counselors that were a part of the system.

David spoke to the receptionist as he walked through the receiving area. It had been such a long time since he had felt rested. Today was a good day. He could almost forget all of the things that had happened last night. Perhaps he would accomplish his tasks today without being sidetracked. He perused the day's schedule that had been conveniently placed on his desk. A few moments later he saw his first clients and advised them in domestic affairs. He saw client after client that day without taking a break. While he offered them good advice that was certainly according to the books, he felt in his heart that there were weightier matters at hand. Not that his concentration was interrupted, but he was compelled to pray for Darlene and her family intermittently that day.

When five o'clock arrived, David found himself driving out to see

Aunt Tillie. Dinner was barely over, according to the schedule posted in the waiting area. At the six o'clock hour, residents would be given a chance to socialize in the activity room or return to their rooms or efficiency apartments. After giving the evening receptionist information, he waited for Aunt Tillie to come down. He was about to start reading again all the literature posted, when the telephone rang at the desk.

"I'll be glad to do that," the receptionist said before hanging up the telephone. "Goodbye" she said. "Miss Tillie has asked that you visit her in her apartment. She's in Number 127, which is down the hall and to the left," she explained while pointing with her long, newly manicured, red nails.

The living quarters were adequate for someone needing care, he observed as he walked. However, he still felt a little depressed at the same time. In one room, he could see two elderly men playing checkers. In another room a woman stared blankly at the television which aired a documentary on desert snakes.

When he turned the corner, he left the individual rooms and now entered small apartments. He was saddened by his next sight. An elderly woman saw him coming in the distance and began to wave at him. He waved back thinking the woman must have mistaken him for someone else. That always happens in nursing homes, he thought. A resident will think a visitor is her child or husband or neighbor.

He was nearly to the elderly woman, when he heard a familiar voice call his name. The voice was coming from the same elderly woman. "David!" the voice said. "How are you baby?" He was shocked as he looked into the eyes of this gentle creature and saw that it was Aunt Tillie.

She aged 10 years without the wig that he was accustomed to seeing. "I hope I didn't scare you without my hair piece," she laughed. "I sent it to the beauty parlor today and they haven't sent it back yet."

"It's good to see you Aunt Tillie," he said changing the subject. He realized she was gray through and through.

"Can we go into your apartment?" he asked.

"Sure," she said, as she wheeled herself in front of him to lead the way. Her apartment was only five feet away. He was pleasantly surprised when he entered. Her apartment was one large room with a sofa, matching chair and coffee table. Behind the sofa was a small kitchen table with 2 chairs, a microwave oven and a small refrigerator. It reminded him an awful lot of his college dormitory room. The only thing missing was the smell of pizza and the noise of the other students.

"Make yourself comfortable," she said, as she wheeled herself around to face him. "Thank God for these two-wheelers," she exclaimed. "If I didn't have this chair, I don't know how I'd get around when my legs get weak. But some days I can stand just fine."

"Were you surprised that I came today?" David asked.

"Not at all," she said. "I've been praying for you all week. The Lord showed me your face when I was in my 5:00 o'clock prayer. Then he took me to the scripture where the Macedonians were praying for help when God sent Paul and Timothy to preach the gospel unto them. I don't know how much help this little old lady can give, but the Lord wants me to try to help you."

David gave her a big hug.

"When we talked before," David said, "there was so much I wanted to share with you. I, I, well, Aunt Tillie, I have a burden on my heart. No matter what I do, it won't go away. At first I thought it was just me. You know, after my parents separated, I was hurt. But I discovered it wasn't just a hurt feeling for myself or my parents. I seemed to have a burden for others going through similar situations. I thought perhaps listening to the problems of other people might have caused it. Then I dismissed that theory because I keep having flashbacks to when I was a child," he said, and paused.

"What happened when you were a child?" asked Aunt Tillie.

"I'm not quite sure how old I was, possibly ten. I had gotten on my knees to pray, at bedtime. Somehow I fell asleep on my knees. The next morning, while we were all having breakfast, I said to my Dad to drive carefully while going to work. Well, he was surprised and asked me why I said that. I answered that he should just be careful. That evening when

I got in from school, Dad was already home. He and mom were sitting down talking. They called me into the room and asked me again why I had asked Dad to be careful. They had such strange looks on their faces that I immediately confessed that while on my knees praying, I overheard a conversation. A voice said "wreck Michael Edwards' car. Another voice answered, "He's one of three cars to be wrecked tomorrow."

"Well Mom started crying and Dad just looked at me, smiled and said, "thanks for the warning son."

"He went on to say that he barely had escaped a horrible accident that morning. After my warning, he prayed when he got in the car that morning that the Lord would protect him as he drove. A car ran a red light and caused two cars to lose control while trying to get out of the way. He was able to swerve out of the way, but one driver was killed and another person was seriously injured. If it hadn't been for my warning, he could have been in the middle of the whole thing. I'll never forget what Dad said to me after that."

"What was that?" asked Aunt Tillie.

He said, "the Lord used you son to save my life," David recalled. "Aunt Tillie, that was the only time anything like that ever happened to me until now. I had really forgotten the incident, but the last few weeks have brought back exactly what I went through then."

Aunt Tillie grabbed David's hands and held them in hers. "It's alright son. You've been chosen by God for a time such as this. That was just a sign of how he would use you later." Tears filled David's eyes as he looked directly at Aunt Tillie.

"Then this makes sense to you?" he asked sincerely.

"It makes perfect sense," she said. "I know you remember the story of a young boy who was anointed by a prophet. Remember it was years later before he actually became king," she explained.

"That's true," said David. "I don't want to question the timing of God," he said. "I've had three dreams that keep recurring," he said. "I actually dream quite often, but there are three that I don't understand. I won't burden you by telling you all three tonight, but I thought you could give me insight on one," he said. "The rest are on this paper. You can read them when you are ready to."

David began to tell the first dream word for word just as he had told it to the pastor. But this time, there was no thunderous laughter, no mocking or hasty answers.

Aunt Tillie looked at him and said, "I'll pray about it." He knew from her tone of voice that she would go to God for answers. He hadn't felt this relieved in a long time. He hugged her tightly and said he would be back whenever she summoned him.

She seemed genuinely glad to help him. Before he left, she laid her hands on his forehead and asked for a special covering from God. "Let your blood cover this young man as he goes forth in the assignment that you've given to him," she prayed. "Don't let him look to the left or the right, but to keep his eyes on you," she continued. "I ask this blessing in Jesus' name." David could feel the presence of God as she prayed. He felt safe, secure and had a feeling that everything was going to be alright.

On the way home he continued to talk to God and meditate on the words of Aunt Tillie's prayer, about not looking to the left or right. It kept ringing in his ears.

He climbed the steps to his apartment and noticed small furniture items in the hallway of his building. There was a lamp and a chair. It was obvious that someone was moving in. He had his key out and was inside his apartment before they returned. "I'll meet them later," he thought. David made preparations to take a shower before eating a microwave dinner. He believed he would sleep well that night and felt very excited about his conversation with Aunt Tillie. He was right. He did sleep well that night.

David awoke the next morning to the sound of a ringing in his ears. He grabbed the alarm to turn it off but realized it wasn't ringing. It was his doorbell. He grabbed his robe, while observing the clock. It was 6:15 a.m. Who would be ringing his doorbell at this hour? he wondered.

Looking through the peep hole, there was a young lady there who looked rather disturbed. David opened the door and said, "good morning."

"Hi," answered the young lady. "I'm terribly sorry to disturb you but we just moved in next door and we haven't had our phone connected yet. I need to call my job and let them know that I won't be in."

"No problem," David said pointing to his phone in the living room. He followed her into the room and turned on the light. She quickly punched in the numbers while apologizing for disturbing him so early.

"Nurses station," she said to whomever answered the phone. "Hi, this is Brenda, I can't come in today because the gas man and the telephone serviceman won't give me a specific time for their arrival. I'm sorry. I hope you can find a replacement for me. I'll be glad to make the time up. I'm sure I'll see you tomorrow. Take care," she said, before hanging up.

"Thank you so much Mr. – ..."

"Oh, I'm David Edwards," he said.

"Mr. Edwards thank you so much for allowing me to intrude at this ridiculous hour. By the way," she said as he opened the door, "We're the McCains; Michael and Brenda. Thanks again for all your help."

David shut the door and stood there in disbelief. Did he hear correctly? Did she say they were the McCains? A strange eerie feeling came over him. He sat down in the nearest chair and pondered what was happening to him.

"Lord Jesus," he said, "Please speak to my heart. I need you to lead and direct my path concerning these people," he prayed.

It was difficult to concentrate as David headed to work that day. David felt as if he was in the middle of a mystery novel. The only problem was that he was the star of the story. He hoped there weren't many clients waiting to see him today. How could he help them? His concentration was not good. "Lord, I know you know how this movie ends," he mumbled as he crossed the parking lot. "I just wish you would tell me."

"Good morning Mr. Edwards," said the receptionist as she glanced quickly at David."

"Good morning," he said, politely returning the greeting. He had not noticed his client Darlene Smith seated on the bench across from the receptionist. When she entered his office a few moments later, he stared as if she had appeared out of nowhere. David hadn't bothered to review his client list. "Good morning Mr. Edwards," she said smiling. "I guess you didn't see me in the lobby by the look on your face."

"No, I didn't," he said, "but please have a seat." "Let's see," he said. "This is your third visit?"

"No, my second," Darlene corrected him.

"Thank you," he said realizing the other visit must have happened in his dreams. "Are things any better for you?" he asked.

She shook her head with disappointment. "I considered not coming back to see you," she admitted, "but I felt compelled to come. After all, the last time I was here I received a big release in my spirit. I guess that is why God made tears," she said smiling. "What's my next step?"

"I need to ask you a series of questions," David said. "Do you believe there are some things in life more important than others?" he asked. She nodded affirmatively. "On a scale of 1 to 10, with 10 being the highest, tell me the number of importance to the following questions. Breakfast," he said.

"Ten," she answered quickly. "Mother always said it was the most important meal of the day."

"I can appreciate your answer, but please do not comment on your number," he said.

"I'm sorry," she said.

"OK, let's continue. Education," said David.

"Ten," she answered.

"Mother."

"Ten."

"Religion."

"Ten."

"A healthy body," he asked.

"Ten," she said again.

"Sleep."

"Ten," she said without hesitation.

"Your favorite pet."

"Ten," she said.

"Marriage," he asked with a little more stress.

"Ten," she answered a little less forceful.

"Thank you," he said while studying his notes. "Would you like to adjust any answers?" he asked.

"No," she said. "Did I pass the test?" she asked after a moment of silence.

"Oh, I just discovered something quite interesting," he said.

"What's that?" she asked looking puzzled.

"It appears that you feel strongly about a lot of issues," he said.

"I certainly do," she said. "It's probably because I was raised that way."

"For example," David continued, "breakfast is as important to you as education."

"Well, if you don't eat a good breakfast, you can't receive a good education," Darlene said, with a chuckle.

David suddenly looked up with a more serious manner. "Breakfast is also as important to you as your marriage."

"That's not true," she blurted out. "You confined me to the scale."

"Did I?" he asked rhetorically.

"Yes. You deliberately limited my answers," she said sounding upset.

"But you had an opportunity to change your answers," he reminded her.

"Well, I had begun so strongly, I felt I should stick to my answers," she said.

"When you discover you're wrong about something, is it hard to admit it?" David asked.

"Sometimes," she said, looking agitated.

"What bothers you more, admitting you're wrong or correcting a situation?" he probed further.

"I'm not sure. Oh well, maybe change," she said adjusting herself in the chair. "I don't like to make unnecessary changes."

"Is it worse, when someone else's changes affect you?" he went further.

"No, it's just change in general," she said.

"How do you respond to necessary change?" he inquired.

"Well it throws me off balance. It interrupts my plans and brings confusion sometimes," she said sounding agitated.

"Does it affect your appetite?" he asked.

"Yes," she said giving in.

"Does it affect your work habits?" David inquired.

"I suppose," she said sounding tired.

"Does it affect your attitude toward others?" he questioned further.

"That depends," she sort of snapped.

"Alright, I know you're tired, but I have one final set of questions that I would like you to answer," he said.

"Alright," she said.

"I want you to put in order of importance the things we've discussed. However, I want you to put them in the order according to what you believe God would want. Start with the least important items. I'll repeat the selections to refresh your memory. Breakfast, education, mother, marriage, religion, your favorite pet, and sleep." he said.

"May I parallel some of the answers?" she asked.

"Sure. They can have the same value number," he said.

"Alright," said Darlene, as she braced herself in the chair. "Breakfast is the least important. Since you used the word religion and not salvation, I'll put education and religion on the same level. Next I'll put healthy body and sleep together. And finally, well, I have to parallel marriage and mother."

"Thank you," David said." That's all I need for today."

"What do you do with that sort of information?" Darlene asked.

"Oh, it helps me to draw some conclusive information about who you are and what your deepest desires may be," he answered.

"Really?" she said. "From that list of information?"

"Absolutely," said David.

"Have a nice weekend," Darlene said as she headed toward the door.

David left work and stopped at the local drive through restaurant. He purchased a burger with a side salad and ate it in the car. He was torn between two decisions. Should he go to visit Rose, or go to see Aunt

Tillie? He was not convinced that Rose was ready to listen to him. He started the motor and headed in the direction of Aunt Tillie's home. He desired answers and he felt a sense of urgency in getting them. Traffic was rather backed up because it was early evening. He stopped at the most convenient supermarket and bought a nice basket of fruit. When he arrived at the facility, he told the receptionist he wanted to see Aunt Tillie in her apartment. The evening receptionist must have recognized him from his earlier visit.

"Mr. Edwards, right?" she said. "That's right," said David.

"Is that for me?" she asked, looking at the tempting fruit basket.

"I wish it were," he said. "I'm sure you deserve one of these."

She picked up the phone and dialed what seemed to be only three numbers. He smiled as he observed her. "Technology is saving us time," he thought. "But what are we doing with the time we're saving?"

She says to come on down," the receptionist said, interrupting his thoughts.

"Thanks," David said. "I'm sure I remember the way."

He carefully lifted the fruit basket and went down the hall carrying it. He loved to bring surprises to people, mainly because he liked to see them happy. He knew that Aunt Tillie deserved to be happy. When he arrived at her door, he knocked twice with his left hand. She opened the door and for a moment he thought he was in the wrong room.

"Don't be frightened," she said. "I just got a new hair piece," Aunt Tillie said, while reaching for a hug.

He hugged her and handed the fruit basket to her.

"Thank you sweetheart," she said. "It looks delicious. Would you put it on my table for me? We need to talk. You kept me up all night."

"I did?" asked David, looking perplexed.

"Yes. I've been praying to God about your situation and last night he unfolded some answers to me. Get me my large print Bible off the end table. I want you to turn to Jeremiah Chapter 25. Read it baby," she said.

David found the chapter and began reading it aloud. "The word came to Jeremiah concerning all the people of Judah in the fourth year of Jehoiakim, the son of Josiah king of Judah, which was the first year of Nebuchadnezzar King of Babylon. So Jeremiah the prophet said to all the people of Judah and to all those living in Jerusalem. For twenty three years from the thirteenth year of Josiah son of Amon king of Judah until this very day, the word of the Lord has come to me and I have spoken to you again and again, but you have not listened.

And though the Lord has sent you all his servants the prophets again and again, you have not listened or paid any attention. They said, Turn now, each of you from your evil ways and your evil practices, and you can stay in the land the Lord gave to you and your fathers for ever and ever. Do not follow other gods to serve and worship them; do not provoke me to anger with what your hands have made. Then I will not harm you. But you did not listen to me declares the Lord and you have provoked me with what your hands have made and you have brought harm to yourselves."

"Alright David," said Aunt Tillie. "That's enough. Now I want you to read Jeremiah 23."

David pulled up a chair and read the whole chapter. He finished it and looked confused.

"David," said Aunt Tillie in a very stern manner. "I believe the Lord is with you. But you will face some strong opposition if you come forward with what the Lord has shown you. You have a message for the people. But you must have a witness. The Bible declares that "out of the mouth of two or three witnesses, let every word be established." You have been given the burden of Jeremiah. His burden was to warn the people of what was to come. If you tell everyone about your dream, some will consider you a false prophet. Just like Jeremiah, you are very passionate about what you have been entrusted with."

"Aunt Tillie," David interrupted, "I already tried to tell someone. They laughed me to scorn."

"You can't let that stop you David," she said. "It was bound to happen. You have been divinely called by God to do a specific work. In order to accomplish it, your prayer life must intensify greatly," she said. "Is your prayer life strong enough to combat the forces of the enemy?"

"Well, I pray and read my Bible," David said.

Aunt Tillie smiled and said, "Baby, you are about to become a prayer warrior. The dreams that God has shown you, cannot be ignored."

"I know," David said. "Because they won't go away."

"You have got to pray until hell itself is shaken by your prayers," she said.

David began to look uneasy and sighed heavily.

"You are going to have to grab a hold to the horns of the altar and pray until you get results."

David was stunned by her words. "By the what, Aunt Tillie?"

"The horns of the altar," she said.

"This is so bizarre," he said thinking about his recent find on the street.

"You may not believe this Aunt Tillie, but I am going to take those words literally."

"Honey, you do whatever it takes, but pray through. It is the only salvation for what you have described in your dream," she admonished him.

"Aunt Tillie?" David asked, "why do you think God chose me? There are so many other people who are ministers and qualified religious people to do his work."

"Baby, God is God. There are certain things about what he does, that he doesn't ask our permission about. One thing is for sure, He knows what's in us. He knows who he can trust and he knows who is trusting in him. Some things He will do for his own good pleasure," she said.

"Yes, I believe he does," David agreed.

"The people you have seen, need your prayers. God did not give you a special burden to make your life miserable. He picked you out because he knows you will be obedient to the call. You have been chosen to help pray these people through their trials. They are not able to see the enemy that is against them, but you are. David are you willing to pray until they get a breakthrough?"

"I believe I am," Aunt Tillie.

"Good, son," she said smiling. "Now hand me that oil from the table."

David passed Aunt Tillie a bottle of anointing oil. He recognized it from the many times his pastor had used it to pray for the congregation.

"Aunt Tillie, before you pray can I ask you something else?" David said. "Why are they targeting three families?" he asked with a puzzled look.

"Oh, that's Satan's way of trying to make a perversion of the trinity," she said matter-of-factly.

"Now David think back, when you saw the demons how were they grouped?"

"They were usually in groups of threes," he replied. "As a matter of fact the more I think about it, they were always grouped in threes. In one of my dreams I clearly was able to identify Discouragement, Disappointment and Dissatisfaction together," he said.

"Well, honey the enemy has always tried to imitate the Trinity," she said. "He wants people to blame God for bad things that happen in threes."

"Really?" said David.

"Oh yes," said Aunt Tillie. "But as the word indicates, we're not ignorant of his devices." When a person accepts the Lord, the Trinity is at work then. They hear the Gospel first. Afterward there's a connection, then conviction and finally conversion. God works in fire and water. In fire there's flame, heat and smoke. The three go together, but they can be manifested separately. In water, there's liquid, ice and steam. The same principle applies. The enemy invests a lot of time in doing negative things in threes, just to confuse people to thinking it's God. And you know what baby, the people give power and attention to the devil by declaring that death and destruction come in threes. They seem to forget that death and life is in the power of the tongue. They'll say something negative and sure enough someone will agree with them. That's why it's so important to know the truth according to the word of the Lord. Every time you hear a negative statement you must combat it with a positive one. That's why you don't hear me saying I'm catching a cold. For the last 30 years, I have always said, I'm catching a healing. Now get down on your knees and let me lay hands on you and anoint you with oil because you have work to do."

As he knelt down she began to use her heavenly language and he felt the atmosphere of the room change with God's presence. Before he left her, he disclosed another one of his dreams to her, knowing she would respond prayerfully.

Chapter Eight

All the way home David felt like the glory of God was hovering above him. He wasn't afraid now of what he would face. He knew from Aunt Tillie's prayer that the blood of Jesus would cover him. He also knew that his prayer life needed to get to a level it had never been. David really wanted to question God, but since he was learning to trust Him in such a great way, he didn't dare ask God why.

David returned to his apartment and listened to his messages. There was a reminder from the dry cleaners, then a message from his sister. She thanked him for being there for her when she needed him most. David used the cordless phone to dial her number, while undressing in his bedroom. It had been a long day, and it appeared that it would be a little longer before David really called it quits.

"Hey Steph," he said, sounding real cheerful.

"Well you must have had a great day," she said. "You sound like it's morning instead of evening."

"Well, what's wrong with evening?" he asked.

"Oh, I don't know, it's just that when the day ends, I sometimes feel it's been wasted. As if I haven't accomplished very much. You know?" she said.

"What are you trying to accomplish?" he asked.

"Are you trying to analyze me?" she said laughing. "I'm your sister not your client."

"No, I'm just curious," he insisted.

"Well, I just want to get my life back on track. I feel like, like, I don't know what I feel," she said.

David was trained in detecting depression. He not only heard it in her voice, he felt it in his spirit. He could feel anger swelling inside of him. He wasn't angry at his sister. He was angry at his parents. He felt powerless but did his best to encourage her to look on the bright side of everything. He almost cried as he spoke with her. Deep in his heart, he knew he didn't see much brightness anywhere he looked.

David was very disturbed when he fell asleep that night. He awakened to the sound of a drum beat. He looked around in the darkness, then drifted off again. The faint sound of a drum was steady and seemed to grow louder and closer. He looked in the distance and saw a group of people marching in a straight line. They were headed to the top of a hill. From where he stood peering, he could see that there were children in the front of the line.

David could see smoke escaping from the mountain, then all of a sudden he saw flames. The children marching seemed to be unaware of the fiery mountain. They were headed directly there. The next thing David saw made him sick to his stomach. An adult ran forward and watched with little emotion as the children passed through the fire. The children went in one by one. The line seemed to be unending. There were screams and then silence. The next person about to go through looked somewhat familiar. He couldn't see the face but there was something about the way she walked.

"Oh no!" he screamed. He reached out to her.

There was a loud thud as David hit the floor. His sheet and covers were tangled. He was weeping. He looked at the bedroom clock and saw that it was 5:03 a.m. He paced the floor for a few moments, then decided he needed to get away from his bedroom and the nightmare that was lingering.

He walked into his spare room and fell on his knees. "Oh God!" he cried with all sincerity, "don't let this tragedy be so." He continued to pray and weep and cry out before God. Then he raised both hands in total submission. He was still weeping when his hands came down. This time they landed on something he could hold on to. His altar replica was directly in front of him. Both his hands grabbed the horns of the altar. It was beyond anything he could reason, but this seemed to give him strength to continue to pray. He prayed and he wept and he prayed some more. He prayed with his prayer language and he prayed with his understanding.

After a while he got up and was much surprised to find that an hour had passed. He felt like he had been to war and had somehow come back with more strength.

◆

Pastor Taylor drove Sister Marie to the church fellowship hall that Saturday afternoon and was a little more quiet than normal.

"You know," he said, carefully turning the corner that led to the church, "I'm a little surprised by David Edwards," he said. "I expected him to have come to his senses by now and patch things up with Rose. I happen to know that he still loves her."

"Perhaps he has some issues that he needs to resolve before the marriage," his wife offered.

"Issues? please," he said, in a condescending way. "Honey these young people don't know about problems like we had when we were young. We lacked money and had to worry about war and..."

"Sweetheart," said Sister Marie, cutting him off, "maybe they don't lack money, but they have a different kind of war. Maybe they are trying to-.."

"Is that what you talk about in your little tea party? I hope it's not just another Tupperware party where you throw in advice on how to keep your home clean," he said with a little chuckle.

"Would that be so wrong if it were?" she said sounding a bit exasperated.

"Oh no, not at all honey," he said realizing he may have hurt her feelings. He reached over and gave her hand a little squeeze. "Whatever you and the ladies are doing is fine with me. Women need good instruction and these women are getting it from the best," he said smiling. "I'm just concerned that David and Rose aren't making wedding plans. I always thought of him as a fine young man for my daughter, but right now, I don't know," he said, as he pulled up and parked in front of the fellowship hall.

"I think if we pray for them and give them time, things will work out for the best," she said.

"That's why I married you," he explained. "You always know just what to say to make me feel better."

He got out of the car and opened her door for her. In the seven years they had been married, he was consistent about this one thing. He knew that she loved for him to open her door.

"That's funny," she said as he assisted her out of the car. "I thought you married me for my money."

He laughed and hugged her. "Are you sure you have a ride home?" he asked. "Yes, I'm sure." she said.

"You're not angry with me for the thoughtless remark I made about the Tupperware, are you?" he asked.

"I wish you'd get out of here," she teased. "There are at least twenty young women impatiently waiting to hear about how to clean their dirty ovens."

She was pleasantly surprised when she walked in the hall to see that everyone who had been invited was already there. She checked her watch to find that she wasn't late. These women who she felt led to counsel, were all early, all anxious and all quiet.

"Hello ladies," she said with a smile. "I'm Sister Marie Taylor, for those of you who don't know. I'm Pastor Taylor's personal cook," she said looking serious. There were giggles and a few uninhibited laughs.

"Now that I know you're not too religious to laugh, I can proceed. I can't tell you how glad I am to see you today. If you don't know the ladies you're seated next to, please introduce yourselves."

This was her second attempt to help the women of her church. This was a totally different crowd than last month. As the talking came to a halt, she stood at the podium and looked around. "There are 22 of us here today. You've been invited by God; I extended the invitation on his behalf. You are here for one of two reasons. You either need to receive or you need to share. That's it. No hidden agendas. No secret club. I love you. I met some of you during the Annual Fellowship. Some of you I don't know very well. Like I said, I just wanted to be obedient and invite you here. At our first meeting, food was served first. I thought I'd reverse that at this meeting."

"By a show of hands, how many of you are married?" she asked. All but two hands were raised. "With children?" she continued. "Your husband is a good provider?" The hands stayed up. "Now, don't raise your hand on this one. How many of you are happy? I don't have to count hands because I can read your spirits," she said.

"You two ladies who aren't married, what are your names?" she asked smiling? "I'm Clarissa," said a rather shy young lady who was noticeably overweight for her height of five feet. "I'm DeBorah," said the other young woman with a voice that you had to strain to hear.

"Thank you for coming ladies," said Sister Marie smiling warmly at them both.

"I need a volunteer," said Sister Marie as she handed some blank paper to a neatly dressed young woman. "What's your name?" Sister Marie asked, standing directly in front of her.

"I'm Nicole Davidson," she answered sweetly.

"Nicole, please give each young lady a sheet of paper. Ladies please raise your hand if you don't have a pencil and Nicole will bring you one of these. Now after you all have received both a pencil and a sheet of paper, raise your hand," she instructed.

One by one the hands went up. Nicole took her seat in the front row.

"You ladies have two minutes to draw a picture of what your idea of the perfect family looks like. Ready, set go," she exclaimed while watching her wristwatch.

The ladies at first looked puzzled, then proceeded to draw circles and other geometrical shapes. Sister Marie began to walk around the room, peering onto the papers as she watched the ladies drawing as quickly as they could.

"Alright, times up!" she said.

"Ladies, please exchange papers. Whoever gets 100 points, gets twenty dollars," she said. "Please write the points in the right hand corner. Alright, if you drew a picture of a lady, ten points. A man - 20 points. A child -ten points for each child. Did anyone draw over 3 children? If one of the children is a baby, another 10 points. OK. A dog, cat or bird, 3 points. A house 10 points.

Alright ladies give yourself 25 points, if you drew a picture of God somewhere in your drawing. There was a possible 108 points that you could have received. Did anyone get 100? Did anyone get 95 or higher? Did anyone get 90 or higher? Did anyone get 85 or higher?" Sister Marie acknowledged the hand of a young lady in the back of the room.

"Great, tell us your name and your score," she said.

"Well," said a rather tall young lady with her hair cut in an attractive style. "My name is Debbie Albright and my score was 86!" she said with excitement.

"Go on and describe your perfect family picture," Sis. Marie said. "OK" said Debbie, I had a picture of a woman, a man, three children, one was a baby, two dogs and a house." The other ladies began to applaud her as she waved the winning paper in the air.

"It's interesting, that no matter how close you all came to 100 points, you all came up short. Just like we will all come up short in life, if we don't add God to our picture. I'm sure that someone in here could have used twenty dollars, but you have to forfeit a blessing, because you did not consider God," she said. There was a sound of murmuring that she couldn't quite make out.

"Does that make you unhappy? Good. Because God is not pleased when we leave him out of our "so called" perfectly happy homes. The sooner we realize this, the sooner we can be a little closer to having real happiness. Now let's get to work."

CHAPTER NINE

David called his mother before leaving to go to the car wash. He also needed to go to the dry cleaners to pick up and drop off his shirts and finally go to the supermarket. That was one chore he dreaded. Thinking about it made him a little sad. He had often imagined he and Rose going together to the supermarket. Now, well he didn't know what would happen. He needed to pick up a few things for his mother. Actually it was one big thing. She had placed a meat order at the butcher's and she was happy that he would carry it to the deep freezer for her. He grabbed his shirts and stuffed them into a pillow case before heading out the door. It only took a couple of minutes to drop them at the dry cleaners. And of course, they always had his shirts ready for him when he got there. That was one of the things he enjoyed about this small city.

His mom's meat order was much smaller than he anticipated. Of course, there were only two of them. With the residue of the morning prayer still fresh in his mind, he brushed off the ever-present reminder of his parent's separation. He would wait to wash his car after dropping off her meat. He didn't want to take a chance in having it spoil, by forgetting to get it out of his trunk. When he pulled in the driveway, he popped the trunk from inside. He was barely out of the car when someone blew their car horn and drove by. He noticed it was his father's car and he waved. His dad's apartment was only a few blocks away. Yet something disturbed David so much that he could barely carry the package. It looked like a woman was on the passenger side of the car. He braced himself. He was just not ready to confront this. He had too many issues of his own. Hopefully, his mother wasn't watching.

Suddenly the side door opened and his mother walked out. "Hi Honey, why did you blow?" she asked.

"It wasn't me," he answered. "Dad was driving by."

"Oh," she said. "Thanks for picking up the meat. Want to come over for dinner tomorrow?"

"That sounds like a good idea," he said following her into the house. "I could use a good Sunday dinner. What are we having?"

"Roast beef of course," she answered. "Would it be Sunday without my roast beef?" she teased him.

"While I'm here," David said, changing the subject, "how's Steph doing?"

His mother seemed to ignore the question as she opened up the waxed paper to inspect the meat. David repeated his question and was taken aback by her response.

"I heard you the first time," she said. "I think Steph is doing the best she can. I, I really don't want to talk about it right now, baby."

"It's alright mom," he said. "I know things are rather tough and you have a lot to deal with."

"Yes, I do," she said in a surprisingly loud tone, as she turned around to face him. "And it's just not fair. It's not fair," she said, with large tears flowing. David quickly went over and hugged his mom. He would have cried with her, but he was relying on the strength he received from that early morning prayer.

"Things will get better," he said. "They have to," he declared by faith.

"Do they?" she asked.

"Yes," he said firmly, looking directly into her puffy face. He could feel anger swelling on the inside of him again. But he was only angry at one person. That person was the devil.

"Don't let me keep you from doing those things you need to do," his mother said. "I know you mentioned the car wash. Go and take care of your business. I'll see you tomorrow," she said wiping her face on her apron.

David played the radio a little louder than normal going home. Washing his car helped him blow off a bit of steam, but he was still angry. He checked his machine for messages upon entering the house. His buddy, Stephen had invited him to a pickup game of basketball at the gym. He hadn't seen Stephen since last month, although they used to talk all the time. At least all the time, by guys standards, which is once or twice a week. Now their jobs kept them too busy to shoot the breeze. Just last year in May, he had been the best man in Stephen's wedding to Myra.

He returned the call and agreed to meet him for a pick-up game that evening.

The autumn sky seemed unusually red with streaks of bluish purple which made it appear surreal. There weren't many cars on the parking lot of the gym. But sometimes when the weather is fair, it's difficult to get the young guys to play inside. It didn't matter to David because he was more interested in seeing his friend. Inside, he could hear the bouncing of a ball and the noise of tennis shoes pounding the gym floor. He ran into the game and tried to take the ball from a rather short guy who was dribbling. Stephen quickly took his eyes off the ball and recognized that David was the one joining the game uninvited. He laughed and grabbed his friend for a hug. They left three young guys to finish the game as they trotted off the court.

"You've lost weight since last month," David said.

"Well, maybe a little," Stephen agreed, as they both sat down in the locker room. It was deserted, so they selected that site to get reacquainted.

"So what's going on with you?" Stephen asked.

"Man you wouldn't believe the things going on in my life. I've postponed my wedding to Rose," he said in a rather melancholy way, while watching Stephen's eyes grow large with surprise. "And right now I'm just seeking God for clear directions. I've never been in a situation like I'm in now. Yet I feel closer to God than I've ever felt. I'm sure later I'll be able to share some things with you."

"Wow!" Stephen remarked. "Oh well, he said matter-of-factly, I guess there's just something in the air."

"What do you mean by that?" asked David.

"Myra and I are having problems," Stephen answered.

"Problems?" David asked.

"I need to be totally honest with you; we're considering a separation," he said, lowering his voice.

David dropped his head as he felt his heart sinking. Here sitting before him, was one of the few friends he admired for having a great marriage. His friends were college sweethearts; career oriented and both steadfast Christians. At least he believed they were. David didn't quite know what to say. He wanted to cry. He loved Myra like a sister. He didn't know if he should probe into their affairs or wait to see if Stephen would voluntarily tell him the situation. This wasn't an office client. This was his dear friend.

"Do you want to talk about it? Because it's ok if you don't."

"I don't mind," Stephen said, "because God is my witness, I don't really know what happened."

"What does Myra say?" asked David.

"She claims that about four months ago, I purposely embarrassed her at a dinner party that we had with some of our friends. I still don't know what I said, because she won't tell me. I apologized, but she says I'm insensitive. Well you know how I like to tease and kid around, I wouldn't do anything to deliberately hurt her, but if you can remember, she never could take a joke," Stephen said.

"Yes, I do remember," said David. "I think it had something to do with the verbal abuse she suffered as a child, from her stepfather."

"What verbal abuse?" Stephen said. "I know her stepfather, he's kind of like me. He likes to tease."

"Didn't she ever tell you that she hates it when he teases her?" David asked. "See, she sort of confided in me one day when we shared a psychology class in college. She said she never felt she could tell him how she hated his teasing her without embarrassing her mother. So she would sort of grin and bear it," David explained.

"Well, we've discussed her family many times, but," he paused as if remembering.

"What is it?" David asked.

"Now that I think about it, every time I mention her stepfather, she either changes the subject or gets an attitude. Whatever the case, I'm at my wits end. I've apologized until I was blue in the face. I don't know how much more of this I can take. I didn't marry her to be miserable and I'm not sleeping in the guest room for the rest of my life. It's gotten ridiculous. I've been there a month. How long can a woman hold a grudge?" he asked throwing his hands up in the air. "I work around a lot of beautiful women and I'm not perfect, so I think she'd better come around to her senses or-"

"Stephen!" David yelled out in the guest locker room. "She's not just holding a grudge. Can't you see her problem is deeper than that?" he said, as he felt the anger swelling up on the inside.

"Well, I'm not a trained psychologist," Stephen said curtly.

"This has nothing to do with being a psychologist. Can't you see you're under attack?" David asked.

"What do you mean by attack?" Stephen asked dumbfoundedly.

"Let me ask you this," David answered. "When was the last time you and Myra prayed together? Not in church but in your home?"

Stephen looked puzzled and was quiet. He stared at the tiled ceiling then looked at the freshly mopped floor. He shook his head in shame when he declared "I don't know that we've ever really prayed together," he said with shamefacedness.

"Would you do me a favor?" David asked. "Don't make any sudden decisions about separating, even if she insists. I'm going to seek the Lord for a remedy to help. You have got to start praying too!"

A tear rolled out of the corner of Stephen's right eye as he grabbed his friend and hugged him. He then quickly left the locker room.

CHAPTER TEN

The alarm didn't awake David the next day in time for his morning prayer. Loud voices and the sound of shattering glass caused him to sit up with a sudden jerk. He couldn't make out clearly what was being said, but he did recognize the voice of his new neighbor. Obviously the apartments were designed so that their bedrooms were just opposite one another. The walls weren't thick enough to control sound. He slowly got out of bed and headed for his prayer room. He really was beginning to love the idea that God was waiting for him each morning, precisely at five o'clock.

David kneeled down at his altar and began giving thanks to God for so many things, especially those he had experienced the day before. The noise grew louder from the next apartment, but he ignored it and continued to give thanks. He then heard an eerie sounding shriek that followed with sobbing. He grabbed hold of the altar and prayed for that couple. He prayed as if their very lives depended on his prayer. Soon after, the sobbing ceased and David prayed for other couples. He prayed for Stephen and Myra and he prayed for Keith and Darlene Smith. He felt he was battling the very forces of evil through his prayer, but he would not release the horns of the altar until he was satisfied that he had gotten through. About an hour later, he left the prayer room and slept lightly for two hours before getting ready for Sunday morning service.

The church service was quite lively on this first Sunday of the month.

The choir seemed more inspirational than he could ever recall. He looked around the sanctuary and noticed that others were also being blessed. He noticed there were more unfamiliar faces than usual. The church announcer approached the microphone.

Welcome to the church where Jesus is Lord. We're so excited that you have joined us for Family and Friends Day," she said. David tuned out everything else that was said after she mentioned family and friends. Where had he been? This was the first mention of that special day that he could recall. Had he known, he would have insisted on being together with his mother and sister. He had not seen them yet, this morning. Perhaps they were in the balcony. He began to feel uneasy. He was hoping that this wouldn't be a big deal throughout the service, because he didn't care for discussing his family right now. A visiting minister stood in the pulpit and talked about how wonderful family life could be. He reminisced his own childhood and familiarized the congregation with the discipline he learned from his parents.

David just sat there and wondered what planet this visiting man of God could have come from. His description of family life sounded closer to the Norman Rockwell picture on the office calendar than anything close to the realities of the day. David got up to leave, right after the offering. He felt he should find his mother. He slowly walked down the aisles toward the door, looking in the section where she usually sat. There was no sign of her attendance. He asked the usher who knew her well, if she was there. The usher said she had not seen her, so he left it at that.

David walked outside the main sanctuary into the church lobby. Someone was coming through the outer door carrying a large bouquet of flowers. It covered their whole face. He knew they couldn't see to open the door so he offered to get it for them. It was only after he opened the door to the sanctuary that he saw that it was Rose. The bouquet she carried said 'Family of the Year' on a yellow ribbon. They stared at one another for a few seconds, yet time seemed to stand still. She then thanked him politely as she went through the door to carry the flowers to her father, who would present them as he always did to the family he felt deserved it.

David drove straight to his mother's home. He knew he would be early for dinner. That was alright with him. Perhaps she wasn't there, but at church after all. He just wanted a refuge, even if she wasn't home. He had a key.

When he arrived, there was no visible sign of her car unless of course it was in the garage. He entered through the side door and there she was dicing onions in the kitchen.

"Hi Baby, you're early," she said. "Didn't you go to church?"

"Oh I went to church alright," he said. "But I couldn't find my mother, so I left." "Oh I knew it was going to be a rather long service because of Family and Friends day," she said. "So I decided not to go. Steph and I did some cleaning that had been put off for various reasons," she explained. David decided to change the subject. He knew his mother well. If she didn't go to church today, it was because it was too painful. She had never put housework in front of her church attendance. He wanted to spare her any further embarrassment.

"Steph and I got a lot of cleaning done," his mother said, as she sautéed the onions in a skillet. "There's a pile of things in the family room. If you want any of it, take it. Otherwise it will be put out for the garbage man."

"Uh oh," said David. "This sounds serious. I might have to rescue some high school trophies," he said, loud enough to be heard throughout the house.

"Steph's not in her room," his mother said. "I sent her to the store to get ice cream."

"Oh," David said, quite amazed by the stuff on the den floor. He went into the kitchen and grabbed a large brown paper bag. "I think I'm going to rescue some of my college books," he said.

"Yea, clutter up your own home," she teased. He grabbed three books, two of them were psychology and one was English. Then his eye caught a large white book that had been well preserved. It was kind of bulky and had a few snapshots hanging out of it. It was his parents' wedding album. A chill went up and down his spine. He didn't open it. He just put it in his grocery bag and continued to look for other hurtful treasures. It wasn't necessary to discuss it. He heard the door opening and saw Steph enter with a small bag.

"Alright, I've got ice cream," she said. "Now we can get on with dinner."

"Not until I rescue all of my high school and college memorabilia," David teased.

"Well, look what the wind blew in," she said.

"And I'm just in time to save my precious heirlooms," he rebutted.

"Huh!" Steph, laughed. "You didn't want that junk when you lived here. Now all of a sudden, you're inseparable. Let's see what you rescued," Steph said, walking toward him.

"No way," he said closing the bag. He pulled the keys from his pocket and headed for the door. "I'm putting these in my trunk now, so no one can reclaim them." When he returned, his mother announced that dinner was ready and they ate in the dining room.

Dinner was a rather sobering experience. He avoided discussing church so he wouldn't have to bring up their theme. He couldn't talk about Rose, that situation was on hold; and he couldn't ask how the two of them were getting along because it was rather depressing. His mother asked about his job, so he discussed non-personal situations from his clients that he thought she'd find interesting.

David was exhausted by the time he arrived home. He pulled out his Bible after he prepared for bed. With only the light from the lamp on his night stand, he began reading a familiar passage. "Think it not strange when you are tried with the fiery darts of the wicked one," it read. Shortly afterward, David's head fell to the side in deep sleep. He was restless and woke up at 2:00 a.m. He thought if he drank some water it would help him rest. He was awfully thirsty, as if he had been in a warm place. He had been dreaming. But he couldn't quite remember his dream. He picked his Bible up and found the passage that he had been reading earlier. Before he knew it, he had fallen asleep again. He continued exactly where he had left off. A barking neighborhood dog must have awakened him. The clock showed 4:15 a.m. He reached over to turn out the light that had been on all night and turned over to continue his sleep. He jumped suddenly when the alarm went off. His right fist was clenched tightly as if he was grabbing something. He opened it. There was nothing there except a small part of his sheet covering. He was perspiring and felt as if he'd been traveling all night. Then he remembered. It was that recurring dream. He shut off the alarm. There was no need to write this one down, he had done so before. He faithfully made his way into the prayer chamber. It was beyond a necessity. It was urgent.

He was thankful after work that day that he didn't have to tell anyone about his weekend. What was there to tell? His life was going through a crisis, and only God could see him through it.

Although he knew he should call first, he didn't bother. After work, he drove directly to Aunt Tillie's and again arrived during the dinner time. He felt bad about interrupting her at meal time and coming empty handed. A few blocks away he had passed a peddler selling pecans. He wasn't sure if she liked them or not. He arrived, parked the car but didn't get out of the car. After pondering, he restarted the engine and went back to get her a bag of the fresh nuts. This would buy him enough time to keep from interrupting her dinner. Inside the building, residents seemed to be returning to their apartments. The receptionist instructed him to proceed to Aunt Tillie's apartment. He thought he heard talking when he knocked on the door. He knew that many elderly left their radios or television sets on for company. He was bracing himself to present the pecans when the door opened. He felt rather embarrassed to find Rose on the other side of the door.

"Are those for me?" she asked, looking at his extended hand with the present.

"Just kidding," she said as he stood there feeling silly. "Aunt Tillie, David's here," Rose said, sounding like an announcer.

"Oh I know honey, he just rang me," she said. "I didn't tell you because I didn't want you to go running out of here," Aunt Tillie continued.

"Me run? I wouldn't do that, Aunt Tillie. That's David's specialty. Besides I was here first," Rose said in a teasing way.

"I'm sorry," David said apologizing to Rose, "I didn't plan to interrupt your visit. I didn't know she had company. I can come back another time," he said, hoping she wouldn't take him up on his offer.

"Oh, it's alright David," Rose said with a smile. "I was just about to leave any way."

"But you don't have to Rose, really. I should have called before coming," he said apologetically.

"No, I have choir rehearsal," she explained as she put on her jacket. "I was just checking up on my favorite lady."

"I don't know what I would do without you baby," Aunt Tillie said. "Be sure to give my love to the family."

"Can I walk you to the car?" David asked.

"That's not necessary," Rose said. "I parked very close to the door and I'm sure Aunt Tillie is ready to visit with you," she continued.

He was about to put up an argument, but Rose held up her hand to stop him. "Please David," she insisted. "It really is ok, we can talk some other time."

"You promise?" he said. "Sure, she smiled. "I always keep my promises."

He wasn't quite sure how she meant that last statement, but he stepped aside. He watched her as she went down the long corridor and around the corner. He then came inside and shut the door.

"I can always come here and feel peaceful," he admitted to Aunt Tillie as he handed the nuts to her. "Thank you baby. I'll save these for a special occasion. How have you been resting?" she asked.

"That's just it, Aunt Tillie. I haven't gotten much rest lately. You remember the dream I told you about, before I left last time? I've had it several more times in bits and pieces. It always ends up the same way," he said.

"The Lord really dealt with me on that one, baby," she said.

"You mean you've gotten an answer?" he asked.

"Oh yes," she said. "I knew this was urgent. What the Lord has shown me is marvelous in my eyes. Repeat the dream to me baby and I'll tell you what God spoke to me, late in the midnight hour."

"Whenever I would go to sleep," David said, "I would show up in the dream in this land where there is a long line of young children. They are headed up a mountain. There are adults standing sort of on the side lines. When they get up this mountain I see smoke and flames. Then an adult sort of coaches them to go through this horrible fire. Most go through against their wishes. Others are so young and trusting, they have no idea where they're being led. Then I can hear the screams of the children once they are led into this horrible flame. I can't really see if any of them are coming out. The smell of the place and the horror is too much for me to witness. I usually wake up at this point."

"David," said Aunt Tillie. "I hope you can bear what I'm about to tell you. I kept praying to the good Lord for an answer. He kept telling me the same thing. I really didn't understand it at first. He kept saying Ahaz. Well I didn't know what Ahaz had to do with it until I read and I read some more. Listen to me closely, baby. Ahaz was a wicked King. He was more wicked than nearly all the Kings of Judah that disobeyed God. He was so wicked that he even sacrificed his own sons. That's right. He caused them to pass through the fire."

"But what has that got to do with my dream?" David asked sincerely.

Aunt Tillie reached over to the coffee table and grabbed her Bible. She pulled out two sheets of paper with notes scribbled on them.

"I asked that very same question. I said, Lord I want to know exactly what you are saying. I don't want to error when I deliver your word. This is what He told me. "Parents who divorce without justification, cause their children to pass through the fire," she said reading directly off the paper.

"Wow!" David exclaimed. "That's really deep."

"There's more," said Aunt Tillie. "The long line of children you saw in your dream, were children of divorce. The adults were their parents who were leading them to be sacrificed. You see baby, there's more to divorce than two people going separate ways. The reasons behind the divorce, are the very things that make it a sin in the eyes of God. In the Old Testament Ahaz sacrificed his sons to serve and appease other gods. He did it in the Valley of Ben Hinnom. You see, to follow after idols, a sacrifice must be made to keep the gods from being angry. You have to know what these gods represented, in order to understand the sacrifice of children. There was Baal in many forms. The name Baal means lord. He was considered a fertility god. He was higher than the other heathen gods. If he conquered the other idol gods in war against him, there would supposedly be seven years of fertility. If he failed, then seven years of drought. So they wanted good crops and cattle. This was their prosperity. I looked in my Bible history books and found that a great number of bones that were dug up in Ben Hinnon Valley years later, belonged to young children. They were found in the valley along with parts of statues that were idols. The idols like Ashereth and Tophet represent lustful pleasures and things that temporarily satisfy the flesh. The children of divorce have been sacrificed for what appears to be prosperity and pleasure. Men and women have become lovers of themselves more than lovers of God. God hates divorce, but do people care? If they think that they can get more pleasure for their flesh by going their own way, they will sacrifice their children in the name of anything."

"But aren't there cases where divorce is allowed?" David asked sincerely.

"Sure there are baby. Jesus specifically talked about those cases. Those are the people who can get in the face of God and say Lord I don't really have a choice. I tried the best that I could. This marriage is destroying me. But I'm here to tell you that not many people have said that in the face of God. He knows if they are divorcing for selfish reasons. If there are children involved, they had better be sure that they have the permission of God to divorce. He is angry when the innocent children are led to the sacrifice, in the name of the god of pleasure.

Now when people who do not know the true and living God divorce, it's not a great surprise, because they were never trusting in God. But baby, I'm here to tell you that Ahaz was not a heathen King. He was King of Judah. The long line of children you saw in your dream were children of Christians. Ahaz let the influence of the heathens cause him to do this great evil. The church has let the influence of Hollywood and wicked movies tell them that they should divorce their partners and find true pleasure elsewhere. Remember David, all that is in the world is the lust of the flesh, the lust of the eye and the pride of life. You can only be influenced by these things if you stop reading God's word and stop praying."

David rested his face in his hands. When he looked up again, he hesitated to speak.

"Aunt Tillie," he said, "Why do you think my Dad left my mother?"

"Oh baby, I'm sure he was having a mid-life crisis. The devil will do whatever he can to break up a Christian home. The church has gotten too comfortable with traditions. We pray as if this is a time of peace. We are in a battle every day. We have to pray before we see the trouble. We're in a silent war. The trouble is, the church is the one silent and the enemy can sneak in easily. The enemy attacked when your father wasn't looking. He was at a point in his life where his prayers and Bible study should have increased. Instead his appetite to satisfy flesh took over. When people are hungry, they will eat anything. The Prophet Hosea says, "They have eaten the Fruit of Lies because they trusted in their own way." Aunt Tillie just shook her head and was quiet for a moment.

David seemed overwhelmed by everything she revealed to him. "Fruit of Lies? Is there really any hope then, Aunt Tillie? I mean what can I do to change the way things are going?"

"Baby, God's not looking for you to save the world, he sent Jesus to do that. But you have an assignment to go after the ones he has shown you," she said.

"What about the children, Aunt Tillie? Lately, I've seen my own sister's face in line to be sacrificed with the others. I keep trying to reach her in the dream," he said with exasperation; "but I'm never close enough. Just when I think I've got her, she - I don't know," he said with a hung down head.

"Baby, don't you know through the Holy Spirit that you have the power to snatch her from the fire?" she said with confidence.

"Honey, remember this," she said looking into his eyes, "a prayer warrior is always one step ahead of the devil."

His deep frown soon turned into a huge smile as he realized and remembered that he had authority over the enemy.

When David left Aunt Tillie's that night, he felt like a soldier who had just completed boot camp. He felt he was ready to do battle. He was determined to set aside his own personal agenda in order to be totally used by God, to accomplish his mission. He could hear the scripture, "I'm confident of this very thing that He that has begun a good work in you will perform it until the day of Jesus Christ."

He tidied up his apartment a bit when he got home. He removed his parent's wedding album from the paper bag and placed it carefully beneath the altar in his prayer room. He didn't know what the outcome was going to be, but he was sure that God was going to do something to turn the hearts of his people around.

CHAPTER ELEVEN

The next work day, there was serious counseling to be done. David would be meeting with Darlene Smith for session three. From the moment she entered his office that Tuesday morning he knew that things had gotten worse. He recognized the spirit of depression by the way she carried herself. Her mood was cooperative but nonchalant. He wanted so much to chase that spirit of depression away, by sharing the love and hope of Jesus Christ. But even though this was a Christian counseling organization, there were limitations placed on spirituality. They also had to clinically treat their patients according to state regulations.

"Are you going to share the results of my test from the last session?" Darlene asked.

"Yes, I am," David said, still closely observing her behavior. "Are you anxious to know my findings?" he asked.

"Well, I just, well, for lack of a better term, want to find a quick fix for my situation," she said.

"That's interesting," David said. "I don't think the situation happened overnight."

"Of course not!" she said defensively.

"Yet, you would like an overnight fix," he continued. She was silent and stared out the window.

David retrieved some papers from his bottom right drawer. "First of all," he said, "you're a loyal wife and a concerned parent. You are a very analytical person," he continued. "Things either work for you or they don't. You like things orderly. You don't stagger in the middle of the road. You like direct answers. You wish people would treat you the way you treat them. You're very proud of your Christian upbringing and the direction you have chosen as a career. You expect two plus two to equal four. You expect hydrogen plus oxygen to produce water and you expect the person you give your love to, to give you back that same love. Am I right so far?" he asked. Darlene nodded her head.

"Yet when conditions are favorable for one result, but they produce something else, you feel your world is falling apart, because that's not the way you were raised. That's not the way you studied it and that's just not fair. You see, Darlene, in a perfect world all things would work correctly and all people would act right. But we live in an imperfect world. Your mind has had some difficulty processing data that doesn't make sense and the reaction has shown through your body's health. Sometimes it's weight loss and sometimes it's weight gain. We can't really fool ourselves into thinking that everything is alright for very long. Our senses are stronger than our bodies. Our intellect is difficult to override. You need to tell yourself the truth no matter how painful it may be. Now that I've given you my official report for the record, may I give you the unofficial report?"

"I don't understand," she said, looking puzzled.

"Darlene, your problem is more spiritual than it is natural. Let me explain," he said standing up and walking to the front of his desk to be closer to her. "Do you believe that God wants your marriage to succeed? Think carefully before you answer."

Her eyes widened and she shifted in her seat as she tried to ponder his question. After a few seconds of silence, she sat up very directly and looked him in the eyes.

"Absolutely," she said.

"Do you believe," asked David, "that there is an enemy who very strongly desires your marriage to fail?"

"I never thought about it that way, but yes I do," she answered.

"Whose side are you leaning on in this war?" he asked her.

"I'm on God's side," she said strongly.

"Then repeat after me. My marriage, come on, my marriage."

"My marriage," she said, repeating after him.

"Will succeed because God wants it to succeed." She repeated his sentence with a new found boldness.

"I can do all things through Christ who strengthens me," David continued.

"I can," she said standing to her feet, "do all things through Christ who strengthens me."

"No weapon formed against me shall prosper," he said, sounding like a preacher.

She repeated his last statement looking up toward the ceiling as if she saw someone there. Then a very large smile appeared, that he had not seen before. "You know what, I feel better," she said.

"If you will continue to confess this," he said, "no matter how the situation appears now or even if it seems to worsen, things will change. Your entire situation will be turned around." She seemed a different person, as she walked out the door. As soon as it closed he threw a punch in the air with his fist and said, "take that devil."

The feelings of victory he cherished for the next few hours were stolen after he returned home. The flashing light of the police car spelled trouble. He wondered what was happening now, as he parked his car and hurried to his apartment. The problem was obviously connected to the new neighbors. David climbed the flight of stairs, not knowing what to expect. All was quiet in the hallways. He put his key in the door just as the officer opened the neighbor's door. He was wearing a badge that read 'Sheriff.' David spoke to him, as their eyes met for that one second. The sheriff said "good evening" and started to descend the flight of stairs. There was no hint of what had summoned him. He would have to wait and ask Brenda the next time he saw her, he thought. Surely she wouldn't mind answering a few questions from her concerned neighbor. He had barely made it to his bedroom, when he heard loud voices. They were muffled but it was obvious that they were angry. He wasn't quite sure what he should do; knock on the door, call the police or pray. Then he remembered that he was in a spiritual war. He quickly undressed and prepared for bed. But instead of going to bed, he went into the prayer room and prayed.

He prayed a fervent prayer for the marriage of the McCains. He also prayed for the Smiths and for his sister. Finally he prayed for his parents. In his prayer, he rebuked the enemy and every device being used against the people of God. He had not eaten since yesterday evening but was not particularly hungry. He was fasting because he knew this would strengthen the prayer life he so desperately needed. He wasn't sure when the voices had calmed down to where he couldn't hear them.

After prayer, he saw that an hour had passed. Although he had worked at the office later than usual, he saw that it was still only 8:30 p.m. He felt forces drawing him to the television but he resisted and grabbed his Bible instead. He clearly heard II Corinthians 4:8 in his spiritual ear. He found the passage and read it aloud.

"We are troubled on every side but not distressed, we are perplexed, but not in despair; Persecuted, but not forsaken; cast down, but not destroyed." Reading aloud helped to drown out the other voice that he heard. The tormenting voice that said, 'why are you choosing to be unhappy?' Who do you think you are? What makes you think God is using you? You can't really make a difference in people's lives. You should be doing things that will make you happy.

He continued to read II Corinthians 4:16-18 and resist the voice. "For which cause we faint not; but though our outward man perish, yet the inward man is renewed day by day. For our light affliction, which is but for a moment, worketh for us a far more exceeding and eternal weight of glory; while we look not at the things which are seen; but at the things which are not seen: for the things which are seen are temporal; but the things which are not seen are eternal."

He was enjoying reading the scriptures as they seemed to add strength to his soul. Yet for some unexplained reason, a great heaviness of sleep overcame him.

David stood to his feet and applauded. His sister's solo was beautiful!

She had sung with such conviction, that she was moved with tears herself. He thought he had heard the song before, but was not sure. Such simple words. "From generation to generation, thou hast been our dwelling place. Will you now restore us with your mercy and your grace? Lord, break we now all images that don't reflect your love, we turn from selfish pleasures and seek Thy face above."

"Sing it again," David shouted. He wasn't sure if she heard him above the applause of the audience. He looked around and saw weary faces now applauding his sister. Both men and women. Her song caused not only applause, but people were dropping to their knees in what appeared to be an open act of repentance. David was shocked. Had this one song brought about a conviction so great that there was a mass repentance? He looked among the crowd for familiar faces.

His eyes continued to search the room until he found someone that looked a lot like his mother. He could only see the profile because she was turned around talking to someone. They were so far in the back that he wasn't sure if they had heard Stephanie's song. David waved his arms in the air to try to get her attention. "You need to hear Steph's song!" he yelled. "Mom, did you hear Steph's song?" Then he began to weep. Exhausted from trying to get his mother to hear Steph's song, he turned again to his sister and said, "Please sing it again." The melodious voice of this teenager again caused a hush over everyone there as she began, "Lord from generation to generation thou hast been our dwelling place." David joined in with his voice to sing the next line.

He sang so loudly that he woke himself up singing. Staring in the darkness at the ceiling, he immediately lost the beautiful melody.

"What were those words?" he whispered into the silence. Not being able to find even a hint of the correct tune, he turned over again and fell back asleep.

Chapter Twelve

David found it difficult to keep his mind focused on his work that next day. He kept trying to remember Steph's song. He had written down the parts he could remember. Every time he thought he had remembered a line, the words just didn't sound right. The song he heard was so sincere, so beautiful, so convicting. He was about to leave for lunch when the phone rang at his desk.

"Mr. Edwards," he answered.

"Hello son, how's it going?" the voice asked on the other end. David was quite surprised to hear this cheerful voice calling him at the office.

"I can't complain," he said. "How are you?"

"Doing great son, listen, have you had lunch yet?" he asked.

"No, I, well no I haven't," David answered hesitantly.

"How about meeting your old man at the diner down the street? I think it's called Cindy's Diner. Hey, it's my treat. I think we're overdo for a talk. Can you meet me there by 12:30? It's a quarter after now."

"Sure Dad," David answered. I'll be glad to see you. Take care."

He hung up the phone and fiddled around the office for about eight minutes. The diner was no more than 6 minutes away, if you walked. David figured walking could do him some good.

When he arrived, his father was already seated at a corner booth that faced the entrance. It was exactly 12:30 and the diner was only half full. Mr. Edwards smiled and beckoned for him to come back there. "Thanks for coming son. I know it was a last minute invitation. How've you been?" he asked in a fatherly tone that was laden with guilt.

"Are you and Rose talking again?"

"We've never stopped talking Dad. We just have some issues that need working out," David explained. "What about you?" David asked.

"Well, your mother and I have been separated about two years now. I thought I should tell you that I'm going to file for divorce soon," he said nervously.

"How soon?" David asked, sensing an urgency in his father's tone.

"Next week," his father answered. "I think it's time to bring this prolonged situation to a halt. We need to move on with the rest of our lives." The words seemed to sting David. He felt numb. He wanted to get up and walk out, but that would be childish. He said nothing at first. He turned his attention to the large picture window and watched the cars go by.

"David, I know this couldn't be a complete shock. After all, we've been separated for two years." David turned to his father and looked him in the eyes.

"Dad, do you think divorce is the answer?" he asked as nicely as he could. However there was a rather sharp edge to his tone.

"Son, I don't know what the answer is, but I can't just continue to live like I'm living. After all, I'm not an old man. I do have some plans for my life that I'd like to follow." He stopped talking, as a waitress approached his table. "What can I get you today?" she asked, while passing them two menus. "The special today is tomato soup with grilled cheese sandwiches and the fruit of the day. It's only $4.50," she said pulling a pad out of her white apron pocket.

"That sounds good to me," the elder Edwards said. "How about you David?"

"I'd just like coffee," he said. "I'm not very hungry."

She scribbled on her pad and asked Mr. Edwards what he'd like to drink.

"I'll have a coke," he said.

"Would your plans happen to include a certain young woman you've been seen with lately?" David asked almost rhetorically.

His father leaned in to get better eye contact with David.

"Alright," he said, "man to man, I think you're mature enough to understand. Melanie and I are in love. We want to get married. She wants to maybe start a family with me. I know I've made some mistakes in the past, but I think things will go better for me, this second time around."

David did his best to hide his anger. Many things were going through his mind, especially Aunt Tillie's words about getting in the face of God. His father knew the Bible as well as anyone. Since they were being so honest, he decided not to hold back.

"Dad," he said in a very calm voice that even surprised his father.

"I'm willing to look over what your divorce will do to mom, to Steph or to me, if you can tell me honestly that you've gotten in the face of God and he has given you permission to remarry and abandon the vows you made to him 28 years ago. If you tell me that God is pleased with your decision, I'll give you my blessing."

The waitress arrived with the coffee and coke just as David stood to leave.

"I'm sorry I won't be staying," he said, as he headed toward the door. His father was too upset to try to stop him. He sat there and stirred his coke with a straw until he could gather his wits about him.

David returned to the office and closed the door. He didn't want to see anyone until he figured out what to do next. Should he tell his mother? No, that wouldn't be wise. Besides it wasn't his place to do it. He would continue to fight the spiritual war with the best weapon he knew about. He would increase his prayers to three times a day. He wished he had someone to talk to, but he was really too ashamed to tell anyone, even Aunt Tillie, that his father said he loved another woman.

Feeling wounded and depressed, David left the office an hour earlier than usual. He went to the supermarket and bought the ingredients for homemade chili. It was really the only recipe he mastered while away at college. Somehow chili always made him feel better.

With a brief case in one hand and a grocery bag in the other, he tried to maneuver the outer door to his apartment building. A young man standing on the inside of the building saw him and came to his rescue.

"Thanks a lot," David said.

"Don't mention it," replied the young man. "I was just standing here waiting for my wife to get home."

"Then we're neighbors," David said. "I'm David Edwards, I met your wife shortly after you moved in."

"Oh yes, she mentioned that. I'm Michael McCain. I was in such a rush that I locked my keys in the car. That's why I'm standing in the hall," he explained.

"Well, you're certainly welcome to wait in my apartment," David offered.

"That will be great. Brenda should be home within the hour," he said. David put the key in the door and let Michael McCain in.

"Make yourself at home," he said as he put the groceries on the kitchen counter. "Don't ask me why, but I'm in the mood for chili," David admitted. "I stopped at the grocer and picked up all the ingredients. I can never quite remember what I have or don't have in my cabinet."

"I'm a fan of chili too," Michael said. "Brenda has a special recipe for making it real spicy."

"She must be a good cook," David said.

"Oh, she's a great cook, when she's got the time to spend in the kitchen," her husband said.

"If you don't mind my asking, how long have you two been married?" David asked.

"Five years; hey you've got nice furniture," he said changing the subject. David knew then that Michael wasn't going to volunteer any information about his private life. He thought he could try another tactic to get him to open up.

"Hey, since you both like chili, why don't you join me for dinner tonight? I always cook enough for at least six, because I never learned to cook for one person," David explained.

"Well, if it's alright with Brenda, it's fine with me," Michael said. "I guess it just depends on how tired she is. Are you much of a sports fan?" Michael inquired, while looking out the window at his car.

"I'm a basketball enthusiast. I also like to shoot hoops at the gym when I can," said David, as he started pulling out a skillet and a pot to start the chili.

"When I was a little younger I used to play a lot with my father," David said; "but that came to a sudden stop."

"Did your Dad die?" asked Michael. "No," said David, "something worse than death. He separated from my mother two years ago."

Michael looked a little stunned. "You mean leaving your mother is worse than dying?" he asked in disbelief.

"Sure," said David. "Dying is something you do when you can't help it. Separation and divorce are both choices you make," he said with confidence.

Michael put the coat down that he had been holding and came closer to the kitchen area.

"So are you saying that you would prefer that your father was dead?"

"Not at all," David said. "What I'm saying is that death is more honorable than the stigma attached to a man who walks out on his family. He can be rich and he can be successful, but somebody, somewhere will always say, I remember when he walked out on his family."

"So what do you suggest a man should do when he can't stand to be married anymore, shoot himself?" They both laughed, just as the onion started to sizzle in the skillet.

"I can only answer from the perspective of a Christian," David said.

"Alright then, what does a Christian man do?" Michael asked.

"Well, it's just my own opinion, but I think a Christian man has to examine himself to see when and where he stopped planting his fruit seeds."

"Fruit seeds?" Michael repeated as if the term was foreign.

"Yes," said David. "In my Bible study at church I learned that there remains two times in the earth: planting time and harvest time. This principle is alive and working in every area of our lives. In marriage, seeds of kindness, forgiveness, longsuffering, etc. are planted. If you stop planting these seeds but continue to need those things, there is a great deficit. Instead of having a bumper crop, you will have a famine and therefore divorce is the only option you will see."

"But doesn't marriage take two individuals who want this healthy crop?" Michael asked.

"Well, I'll put it this way," David said. "The harvest comes much easier and faster when one plants and one waters. But that's where faith and steadfastness comes in. You've got to be willing to plant and water too, if necessary, to keep your marriage alive. But that takes work and patience and many couples choose not to invest in their marriage because there are other options available."

"Did I ask you what you do for a living?" Michael asked. "You must be a minister."

"No, I'm a Christian counselor," David said.

"Well, that explains your wealth of knowledge. I'm a high school administrator," Michael said.

"Hey, that looks like Brenda's car. I'll check with her about dinner," he said, as he grabbed his coat.

"Thanks for letting me hangout."

The door closed and David could hear their muffled voices in the hallway. He dropped his head and said a prayer of thanksgiving. Not only had a door been suddenly opened, but for the last few minutes he had been able to start to minister in a way he had not done before. He was pretty sure they would be back for a chili dinner, but he had so much more to offer them than spicy beans and beef.

CHAPTER THIRTEEN

Dinner was not quite the same in the Taylor household this week day evening. While most of the talking lately had been done by Sister Marie, even she seemed noticeably distracted. Before Rose's breakup with David, she kept her Dad and stepmother abreast of her plans to have a simple wedding with an elegant reception. She'd bring magazines to the dinner table with the latest fashions and she would ask their opinion on certain wedding traditions. Since the breakup, she talked more about the weather than anything personal. It was quite apparent that her private life was not to be discussed.

Pastor Taylor always ate engrossed in deep thought about the next sermon or an organizational meeting.

"What's on your mind tonight honey?" he said, without looking up, as he carefully cut his chicken breast into small bite sized pieces.

"Nothing," answered Rose.

He smiled at his daughter sweetly as he replied, "I wasn't talking about you sweetheart."

"Oh," she said, with a giggle that hid her embarrassment.

"I've just been a little confused about the fellowship meetings that have been taking place," Sister Marie said, stabbing at her overcooked broccoli.

"I thought you said the meetings had been very productive," he said in an interrogative way.

"Oh they have," she quickly responded. "It's not the meeting that concerns me as much as the people who attend them."

"Wait a minute honey," he said. "You told me yourself that the people were hand-picked by you. How can there be a problem, if you invited them?"

"Honey, I told you in the beginning that this ministry was birthed out of a word that came to me in prayer. The Lord had me to hand pick all married women but two. I'm just still wondering why He included the two single women."

"Maybe they're engaged," Rose said.

"No, I kind of doubt that, after talking with them in the meeting," Sister Marie said.

"Well we could suggest answers from now until next week and still not figure out God's mind," Pastor Taylor said. "The Lord works in mysterious ways. When is your next meeting taking place?" he asked.

"Saturday at eleven," she answered. "I sure would like to be a fly on the wall at one of those meetings," the pastor quipped.

"That's just too bad honey because these meetings are for women only, with no exceptions," she said laughing. "You'll have to start a club of your own."

"Somehow, I find it difficult to imagine Dad as a member of anybody's club," Rose said.

"What's so strange about imagining me in a club?" he asked.

"You speak whatever is on your mind Dad," Rose said. "Clubs don't like that. They want you to be in agreement with the way the entire body feels," she explained.

"Maybe that's why God called me to preach," he said. "I don't have to agree with anyone except God."

"How do you know, you're always agreeing with him?" Rose asked.

"By His Word, honey. I always have to line up with His Word," he said, as he pushed his chair back to get up. "Dinner was delicious honey," he said, giving his usual official blessing of what he had eaten before leaving the room. He always finished dinner first.

Sister Marie turned her attention to Rose. "How's your chicken, Rose?" she asked.

"Oh it's very good," she answered, although she had picked at it throughout the meal.

"How do you like the potatoes?" Sister Marie asked.

"They are very tasty and so is the broccoli and the corn bread. I think I've lived with you long enough to know that you have something you want to say to me and I'm sure that it has nothing to do with tonight's dinner," she said, putting down her fork to look directly at Sister Marie.

"Alright, you're much smarter than I give you credit for. I'd like to invite you to this Saturday's women's fellowship."

"Alright, I'll be there," she said. "Don't faint from shock. I know you expected me to give you a hard time. But I know if I said no, you wouldn't give up, because as you put it, you are on a mission or you heard from God or something like that. I'll come so I can get it over with."

"Thanks Rose," she said as she started clearing the table. "You just made my mission a little easier."

When Friday came, David's routine was just a little different. He awoke before his alarm went off, probably because he hadn't slept well. He hadn't dreamed, or at least he didn't remember any. There was just so much on his mind. His father's plans, his sister's song and his neighbor's situation. He was still ecstatic about them joining him for that chili dinner. It was even more productive than he had hoped, since they disclosed that they had a few marital concerns. He was careful not to push too hard, as he tried to generalize about how he had counseled people who were in similar situations. He knew he couldn't take any credit for any of the things that had been happening in his favor.

During his hour of prayer, he now specifically prayed for the debt that was plaguing his neighbors and adding to their problems. They told him they had lost their home and had to move into the apartment until they could again get financially stable. Neither of them seemed to remember when they got above their heads in purchases. David couldn't tell them, but he knew that it was when they were told they probably wouldn't have children that the trouble started. They had borrowed money to travel to a number of exotic and fancy vacation spots. He found it interesting that the subject of children never came up. There are only so many things that you will tell a stranger.

It seemed his hour of prayer was getting more specific each day. Yet it was a sweet hour, because there was something humbling about praying for the needs of others. He felt compelled, even driven, to stand in the gap for hurting people, in spite of the fact that he was hurting too. Yet, after prayer, he always left his room with a sense of being sustained by nothing less than the power of Jesus Christ.

Today he opened his Bible and his eyes fell on Daniel 2:28. *But there is a God in heaven that revealeth secrets, and maketh known to the King Nebuchadnezzar what shall be in the latter days. Thy dream and the visions of thy head upon thy bed are these; As for thee, O King, thy thoughts came into thy mind upon thy bed, what should come to pass hereafter: and he that revealeth secrets maketh known to thee what shall come to pass.*

David closed the book and returned to his bed to meditate on the passage. It was nearly time to get up and prepare for work. Just as he closed his eyes, the telephone rang. Startled by the piercing of the silence, he jumped up and grabbed the receiver.

"Hello," he said wondering with anticipation who would respond on the other end.

"David, it's Dad," the voice said. "I hope I didn't wake you."

"No, I was awake. Is there something wrong?" David asked.

"Well, I'm fine physically, I just haven't slept much since our lunch meeting. I think I was too upset to call you the first couple of days. I keep thinking about what you said to me, about discussing my plans with God. I'm not saying one way or another what I'm going to do," he said.

"Well Dad,"

"Please son, just let me finish," Mr. Edwards said, interrupting him.

"I remember that when you were a little boy you told me about a dream that helped to save my life. Well, this time, I'm having the dream. Almost every night this week I've dreamed the same thing. I go to visit my special friend and I give her a gift. She opens this package that's neatly wrapped and inside there's a bundle of money. I expect her to be thrilled. But instead she looks at the money and gives it back to me. On another night, I dreamed that I was taking her shopping and I tried to give her a lot of money. She gives it back to me. I've dreamed this same dream at least three nights. Look, I don't want anyone to know about this. I just want you to pray for the understanding. I'm sorry to call you so early but I just can't seem to rest with this on my mind. I'll talk to you later. Goodbye."

"Goodbye," David said. He was astounded. While he had been praying sincerely for his father, he never expected this result. He didn't want to chance telling his father his own insight, so he decided to fast that day. It wouldn't be easy because he had a full load of clients to see. Yet, to get a word from the Lord would be worth it.

CHAPTER FOURTEEN

Darlene used the microwave oven to warm the baby's food. She was not especially hungry at the moment because of her late lunch. She figured Keith could have the leftover meat loaf along with fruit salad when he got home. He seemed to be consistently late for the past few weeks. But that was alright, because she had a strange sense of peace. Ever since she began making her confessions, things went from bad to worse. Yet she seemed in control. A month ago, she might have reacted with a loss of appetite, but this time she was steadier in her home and on the job. She also seemed to delight more in Janie. Every day that she picked her up from her mom's, she could hardly wait to get her home and play with her. She wished she could spend most of her time with her, but that was not feasible right now.

The buzzer went off on the microwave just as the telephone rang. "Hello," she answered in sort of a hurry as she reached into the microwave to pull out Janie's food.

"May I speak with Mrs. Darlene Smith?" a voice asked, above light static in the background.

"This is she."

"Mrs. Smith, my name is Lieutenant Bob Richardson of the County Police Department. Is your husband's name Keith Smith?"

"Yes it is," Darlene answered nervously.

"Mrs. Smith, I regret to inform you that your husband has been involved in a traffic accident. Can you come to the County Hospital as soon as possible?"

"What? My, Oh my God!" she stammered. "Is he ok?" she said, fighting back the tears.

"Ma'am, I really don't have the details on his condition," the officer said as comforting as he could. "If you can't drive, we can send a car for you shortly."

"No, I'll drive," Darlene said in almost a whisper. It'll just take me a few minutes to get myself together."

"Just come to the emergency room of the County Hospital. Do you know how to get here?" he asked.

"Yes, I do," she said, leaning on the refrigerator. "I'll be right there, goodbye."

Darlene called her mother as soon as she hung up, and told her the situation. Her mother offered to go with Darlene, but Darlene insisted on going alone. She would take Janie to her mother's and still be only 10 minutes away.

She prayed all the way to the hospital, that he would still be alive. Rushing into the hospital, she pushed through two large swinging doors that seemed to squeak with an unnerving sound. Darlene followed a long red arrow that was painted on the wall that read "Emergency Room."

A young lady sat at a computer with doctors & nurses moving busily around her. "Excuse me, my name is Darlene Smith, is my husband here?" she asked, nearly out of breath.

What's your husband's name ma'am?" the receptionist asked.

"Um it's Keith, Keith Smith, he was in a car accident."

"Oh," the receptionist said, with a strange look on her face. "Just a moment, I'll get Dr. Jones, he's the attending physician."

"Is he OK?" Darlene asked.

"Dr. Jones will answer all of your questions Mrs. Smith." The receptionist dialed two numbers and paged Dr. Jones over the telephone. In about two minutes a short and slightly overweight man with a stethoscope about his neck entered the room. His wandering eyes found Darlene.

"Are you Mrs. Smith?" he asked.

"Yes, yes I am," she said.

"I'm Dr. Jones the attending physician," he announced.

"Where's my husband? How bad is he hurt?" she asked with her eyes filling with tears.

"Calm down Mrs. Smith," the doctor said, trying to avoid an overly emotional situation. "Your husband sustained a head injury when he was thrown from the car. Unfortunately, he was not wearing a seat belt." Darlene hid her face in her hands and let the tears flow.

"Will he be alright?" she said, sobbing.

"It's really too early to give the prognosis, but we're watching him very closely," he said. "Unfortunately, the driver received head lacerations and broken ribs due to the steering wheel," he said. Darlene slowly raised her head and wiped her eyes as she listened to the doctor explain that Keith was not alone.

"Who was driving, doctor?" she asked with great expectancy.

"A Miss Nichols was behind the wheel. Is she a friend of the family?" he inquired.

"No, she's a friend of my husband," she explained.

"How is she doing?" Darlene asked out of curiosity.

"She's stable," the doctor said. "Her sister is with her now."

"How bad is my husband's head injury?"

"He's in what we believe to be a temporary coma," he said.

"Were there other cars involved?" Darlene asked him, as she pulled tissue from her purse.

"No, it appeared they hit a light pole trying to avoid another car," according to the report I heard from the officer.

"Can I see him now?" she asked.

"Yes, you may, but remember he can't respond," he cautioned. Sometimes it helps when you talk to them in this condition, as long as you are reassuring."

She stood up to follow the doctor to a room where a sign read Intensive Care Unit. She could hear the sounds of machines beeping, while working to perform the functions of a body that was unaware of its surroundings.

Dr. Jones pulled a chair up for her to be seated. There were so many things that came to her, as she observed the bandaged head of her husband. It was only five years ago that they were dating. Keith had not been a Christian very long when they met. He was just getting over a nasty divorce from a marriage that hadn't lasted a year. When he met Darlene he had given his life to Christ and prayed for a Christian wife. They had only dated twice before he confessed his love for her and asked her to be his wife. He said he knew that God had put them together.

She tried to remember when things started going wrong. She couldn't. They had been so thrilled to have their first child. He adored Janie from birth. But somehow when she wasn't looking, he started to wander. Since her last session with David Edwards, she had continued to make positive confessions. She would pray specifically for her husband and not against him. Now this.

"Lord, how much more can I take?" she whispered. She reached over to grab Keith's hand and prayed for his recovery. She included her confession in her prayer. "God wants my marriage to succeed. In Jesus' name. Amen."

◆

The counseling center was buzzing with people keeping their bi-monthly appointments. David hadn't had a break all morning. He had one more client before taking his lunch break. He planned to take a walk to help rejuvenate his strength, during his break.

The receptionist knocked at the office door. "You have a cancellation Mr. Edwards," she said. "Darlene Smith just called. She said something about her husband was in an accident and she needs to cancel her appointment."

"Is that right?" David said rhetorically. "How is he?" he asked.

"I'm not sure, but it didn't sound too good," she said.

EATING THE FRUIT OF LIES

"Thank you for the information. I need you to hold my calls until my two o'clock client shows," he said.

He locked his office door and got down on his knees. His life was about to increase to three specific times set aside for prayer. He prayed for exactly one hour both in tongues and for the particular needs that he was now made aware. He refused to feel defeated. He was going to fight the enemy with his faith. He didn't care how bad things were looking for Keith Smith, God was still in charge of this situation. He prayed for his father. He knew that God would give him the answer to the dream. He prayed for all the others that he had been given a burden for, as well. After his hour of prayer, he thought he would rest at his table.

He pulled his Bible out of the bottom left drawer and read from the 55th Psalm." Evening, and morning, and at noon, will I pray, and cry aloud: and he shall hear my voice.

Afterward, he put his head down to rest and soon fell asleep. He would have continued to sleep but he was awakened by the ringing of a telephone.

"Hello," he answered.

"Your two o'clock appointment is here, Mr. Edwards."

"Thank you," he said smiling. "Give me about 3 minutes before you send them in," he requested. He grabbed his pen and pad and wrote down everything he could remember about his dream. He then unlocked the door and greeted his next client.

David went to the County Hospital after work. He found Darlene in the family waiting room with her head back in a meditative position.

"Hello Darlene," he said.

She opened her eyes and smiled warmly. Her gratitude of his visit was evident in her eyes.

"I just wanted to let you know that everything's going to be alright. I've been praying for your husband. I want you to try not to worry, and to keep exercising your faith," he said.

"Thank you for coming," she said, as she got up to hug David. "I believe everything will work out alright. I want you to know that I'm continuing my confession."

"Good," said David, "because the enemy wants you to give up on your husband."

"I refuse to do it," she said.

"Is there anything I can do for you, specifically?" he asked.

"Would you pray with me now?" she asked.

David reached for her hands and held them both, as he bowed his head and gave a prayer of thanksgiving for the life of her husband and their bright future as a family together. He then promised to call and check on her later. He hurried home because he had an important phone call to make.

When he got home, he opened a can of vegetable soup, and made a double decker ham sandwich. He ate a little slower than he thought he would, as he recalled the different things that had happened during the day. He was so thrilled to have an answer to his father's dream. He was a little apprehensive regarding whether his father would accept the answer. Yet he was sure that he had heard from God. After checking to be sure that no one had left a message on his machine, he called his father's apartment. A female voice answered the phone.

"Hello is my dad there?" David asked. He was a bit disturbed that a woman answered.

"Sure," the woman said. "He just stepped into the hall to check his mail."

"Oh," David said. "Would you have him call me later when he's free?"

"If you hold on I'm sure he'll talk to you now," she said.

"Thanks, but I'd prefer he called when he's not busy. Just tell him his son will be available this evening. Thanks."

"Goodbye," she said."

"Bye," David said. He shook his head quickly, as if that would erase her high pitched voice from his mind.

David looked up the phone number for Aunt Tillie. He needed to talk with her and report on all the things that had happened. He called her number and the telephone seemed to ring an excessively long time. He was sure it was because he was so anxious to share all the news.

"Hello," a voice answered that sounded as if it was just awakened.

Aunt Tillie?" David asked.

"Oh, hello love," she said.

"Aunt Tillie, I'm sorry to wake you, I had no idea you'd be asleep by seven o'clock.

"That's alright dear," she said. "Lately I've been catching a healing again."

"Aunt Tillie, I've got so much to share with you," he said.

"Can you come over tonight?" she asked. "I've got something for you."

"Oh, I'm sorry I can't come tonight, but I'll come tomorrow," he promised. "See Aunt Tillie, Dad's going to call me back. He called me the other day and asked me to pray for him. He told me not to tell anyone about his dream that he keeps having, so I couldn't tell you, but Aunt Tillie, I fasted and prayed and God has given me an answer to his dream."

"That's wonderful, baby," she said. "You're growing in the Lord. He's got great things for you child, just keep seeking his face."

"Aunt Tillie, I've got another dream that I will share with you tomorrow concerning my sister. But I'll let you go and get your rest because you sound tired," he explained.

"I love you baby," she said.

"I love you too Aunt Tillie, Goodbye." "Goodbye, love." He smiled as he hung up the telephone. He didn't know a sweeter saint. David began to put his dishes in the sink when the telephone rang. "Hello," he answered cheerfully.

"Hi Dave, it's Dad."

"Hi Dad," he said. "Are you alone?"

"Oh yes, Melanie is gone, she just dropped by to bring me a fruitcake. She's a very good cook," he said, hoping to lighten the conversation.

"That's nice," David said. "I just want you to know that I prayed about your dream."

"I knew you would son. Did you get an answer?" he asked his son rather slowly.

"Yes, I did. Dad remember how you were trying to give Melanie money in your dream?" David asked.

"Yes," his father answered.

"Well," David continued, "the reason she couldn't accept the money you were giving her is because it was counterfeit."

"What do you mean by that?" his father asked.

"Well Dad, in your dream you're certainly sincere about giving her the money to buy things, but you don't realize that the money is counterfeit. She wants to take it because it looks good, but even she knows that she can't spend counterfeit money. And the money represents your love for her. You're basing love on feelings. You feel it's sincere, but God has examined what you feel and has determined that it's only a feeling. Real love is not based on feelings alone. Feelings will change, but love is so much deeper than fleshly feelings. God is love and that's the kind of commitment he wants us to make - the kind based on his steadfast love toward us. I didn't really understand this until I had a dream myself this afternoon. I dreamed that I threw away my watch. As soon as I threw it away I was sorry. I said to myself why did I throw away my watch? It didn't work anymore, but I knew that it only needed a battery. The watch represented time and time is an investment. Dad you invested many years in your marriage. I'm not saying this because I'm your son, I'm saying it because this is the answer God gave to me. You can throw your marriage away, but one day you will regretfully discover that it only needed a battery. So you have a choice, get a battery for your marriage or present your new wife with counterfeit love. I don't have a battery for you, but I know where you can get one," he said. There was a brief moment of silence that seemed to last for an eternity.

"Thanks son," his father said. "Goodnight."

"Goodnight Dad."

David could feel in his spirit that the enemy would do all he could to keep his father from accepting the dreams meaning. He wasted no time.

Instead of waiting until bedtime, he immediately went into the prayer room. Warriors have to be prepared to fight at all times. He didn't just walk into the prayer room. He was driven. His very appetite called for prayer. Yet each time he entered the room to pray was a new experience with God. He felt God calling him to a level that seemed way beyond his comprehension. After all, who was he? He was not the son of a minister. He was not even certain what his gift was in the body of Christ. Yet, somehow in this very room he was being shaped and developed to become a faithful and proven prayer warrior.

His sleep that night was troubled. He sensed something in his spirit, but did not understand how to pray. Intermingled in his dream was Stephanie's song. The bits and pieces that he heard made him feel both happy and sad. Finally the alarm went off. It was time to again seek the face of God.

CHAPTER FIFTEEN

Darlene again sat up all night hoping against hope that Keith would soon awake. She stood up from the uncomfortable hospital chair and stretched.

"Thank you Jesus" she said, extending her arms. She was about to be seated again when she looked down and saw that Keith's mouth was moving.

"Keith!" she exclaimed in a loud whisper. "Oh my God, Keith!" she said a little louder. She moved in closer and called his name a little louder. Almost impulsively she sprang up and ran out of the room to find the doctor.

"He's waking up!" she said excitedly to the nurse at the nurse's station. "My husband is coming out of his coma!" The nurse quickly dropped her paperwork on the table and ran to the room, following Darlene. When they returned, Keith was muttering something they could not understand. The nurse took his pulse, smiled and left to get the doctor. Darlene pulled her chair up closer and held his hand. "Keith sweetheart, open your eyes. If you can hear me open your eyes," she repeated. She started to cry. She wiped her tears and placed her wet hand in his hand. He opened his eyes.

"Home again," he whispered. "I want to go home again." "Sure, I'll take you home," Darlene answered.

"I want to go home with my family; where's my family?" he asked.

Darlene realized that he was not aware that she was there. The doctor came in with an assistant to check him over. When he heard Keith muttering, he took his temperature and checked his vision.

"He's delirious," the doctor said. "He's not yet aware of our presence. But the important thing is that he's not comatose any longer. The delirium will in all likeliness only last for a few hours. Why don't you get some rest?" he told Darlene. "I'll alert you when he's coherent," the doctor said.

"Thanks anyway Doctor, but I'd rather not leave my husband," she insisted.

"I understand," the Doctor said. "Just give me a few moments to check his vital signs."

Darlene stepped aside to the other part of the hospital room. She was so excited she didn't know what to do. A humongous smile filled her face as she looked up and acknowledged God. "Lord, I thank you so much," she said, not caring that the medical team was listening.

"Dar -lene, Dar-lene," she heard Keith call out. She quickly ran back to his side.

"I'm here baby," she said.

He was starting to perspire on his forehead. She grabbed his hand and held it as tightly as she could. She was hoping he would squeeze her hand back. But without her holding it, his hand fell limp like a dish cloth. Keith closed his eyes and fell back asleep.

"It may be some time before he's coherent, but if you insist on staying, just let me know if you see a significant change," the doctor said. "The nurses will be right down the hall," he assured her.

Darlene pulled a Gideon's Bible from out of the hospital drawer and began to read aloud to him. The passage she selected was Psalm 23.

"And I will dwell in the house of the Lord forever. The Lord wants my marriage to be successful. No weapon formed against me shall prosper," she said as she closed the book.

Keith appeared to be resting comfortably. Darlene took the opportunity to call her mother from the telephone in the waiting room. Her mother was quite relieved to hear the progress of Keith. Darlene could hear Janie in the background. She thought it best not to talk to her because she didn't want to upset her. She promised to call back later with news of any changes regarding his condition. She did her best not to think about the accident or the circumstances surrounding it. She wanted to concentrate on her husband's recuperating.

When she entered the room again, Keith's eyes were open again, but this time he was following her with his eyes. She ran to his side and they both wept together. "I need to tell you what happened," he said in a voice a little louder than a whisper.

"No, tell me later when you're better. Save your strength. I have to get the doctor."

"No Darlene," he insisted while holding her hand. "Please listen to me." She sat in the chair and bent her head close to his.

"God has spoken to me," he said with a strange look on his face. Darlene thought he was still delirious and tried to get up again to get the doctor.

"No, please listen to what I have to say," he insisted. "I've just had an experience with God. He told me some things about myself. Things I thought didn't matter. I had my own ideas about marriage and they were all wrong. I wanted our marriage to be what I had in mind for it to be. My motives were selfish. I thought after my first marriage failed that I wouldn't make the same mistakes as before. I wanted to be in control. I know now that I was wrong. I could hear the voice of Jesus talking to me. He said that he designed marriage to be a reflection of his relationship to his church. That's when I knew I'd have to ask you to forgive me. I was way off course." He paused for a moment to get his breath.

"Christ is always loving and caring and forgiving, no matter how the other person is. I've been selfish and stupid. I guess you know I've been seeing another woman...and Darlene, it had nothing to do with you. You've been wonderful. I love you and Janie so much," he said, with tears streaming down his face. "I don't know why I was pursuing someone else. I was coming close to having an affair for no reason at all. That's why I'm asking you to forgive me Darlene. If you can trust me with another chance, I promise to treat you in a way that would make you proud to have me for your husband. I'm just ashamed of myself right now for not being able to face my dreadful past with you. I was always trying to escape my hurtful past. The fact that my ex-wife left me for another person, was still a hurtful memory. I didn't want to talk to you about it because, it really wasn't your problem. It was mine. So if you can just find it in your heart to forgive me Darlene, with the Lord's help I-.."

"You don't have to ask me to forgive you again Keith," Darlene interrupted. "I forgive you and I forgive your lady friend too. By the way, the doctor says she'll be alright, she has a few broken ribs. I believe in my heart Keith that God wants our marriage to be successful," she said smiling.

"I thought I was dead after hitting the pole or whatever I hit," he said. "But Jesus appeared and held out his hand for my hand. He said to me, 'I have a covenant with you.' Then he told me I had to make a covenant with you Darlene. Just as he is my covering. I must be your covering." He paused for a moment and rubbed his head. "But the last thing he said to me," Keith continued in almost a whisper, "was that I had to show Janie how much God loved her by showing Janie how much I love you." At that moment the doctor walked in and Darlene stood up to wipe the tears from her cheeks.

"He's going to be just fine, Doctor," she said with enthusiasm. "I know he's going to be just fine."

CHAPTER SIXTEEN

When David left his prayer room that morning he felt fortified with the strength of God. The scripture he read for his daily devotion was 1 Peter 4:12,13: Beloved think it not strange concerning the fiery trial which is to try you, as though some strange thing happened unto you: But rejoice, inasmuch as ye are partakers of Christ's sufferings; that, when his glory shall be revealed, ye may be glad also with exceeding joy.

He prayed a special prayer that morning for Keith. He couldn't explain it, but he had a special peace after his prayer, even greater than before. He would keep a sacred consecration in his heart that day.

One thing he knew for certain, the burden on his heart was God-given and it could not be ignored. Yet it could be chiseled away; one prayer at a time. After all, there was some progress he could not deny. He had spoken man to man with his father and he was able to tell him the simple truth. It was days like this that he needed to talk to someone. That someone was Aunt Tillie and thank God, he thought to himself, she's expecting me.

Work went rather quickly that day. David's attention was pretty well focused on the report he would give Aunt Tillie. Just like she had prayed, he felt like he had become a prayer warrior. He didn't intend to brag, but he hoped she would be godly proud of him. After saying good evening to the co-workers he headed in the direction of Aunt Tillies' home. Three miles away he stopped for flowers. He never wanted to visit empty handed. The selection of lavender and pink silk flowers were arranged so beautifully over the greenery. He didn't consider himself frugal but he thought they would last longer.

David casually entered the lobby and discovered the receptionist was not at her desk. As a matter of fact, no one else was waiting at that time. He decided this was his chance to knock at her door and surprise her with a beautiful bouquet. The corridor was quieter than normal, considering the dinner hour was just recently ended. Two residents gave him the usual strange stare as he progressed down the hall.

When he arrived at Aunt Tillie's apartment, the door was ajar. He could see the back of someone who appeared to be leaving. The lady turned and faced him when she realized someone was behind her. "Oh hello David," a rather strange sounding voice said.

"Hi Sister Marie, I'm surprised to see you here. Are you coming or going?" he asked.

"I was just leaving," she said. "I guess Rose called you - or maybe not," she said noticing the flowers in his hand.

"No, Rose hasn't called me," he said, "but then again, I haven't been home to check messages. I needed to see Aunt Tillie about something."

Sister Marie grabbed his arm and gently pulled him inside the apartment. "Aunt Tillie's not here, David," she said somberly. "She went home today."

"She's gone back to her house?" he asked innocently.

"No, David. She's gone to her heavenly home," Sister Marie said.

She had barely finished the sentence when she put her hand over her mouth to muffle any sound of expressed grief. She had held up very well that day. However, listening to her own words was a bit too much to bear. David stood there as if someone had knocked the wind out of him. His young face instantly changed to show disbelief.

"She's gone?" he whispered, as if he didn't believe his ears.

"What happened?" David asked, as if there might have been a mistake. "I just spoke with her last night."

"She died peacefully in her sleep," Sister Marie said as the tears began to flow. She went over to David and put her arms around him.

"I know it's a shock, David, but the Lord knows best."

"What am I going to do now?" he asked, as if he was desperate for a friend. He wanted to cry but tears would not come. He sat down on the familiar sofa to get a hold of what he had just heard.

"I know she was special to you David. She often told me so," Sister Marie said, trying to console him.

"She did?" he said in bewilderment.

"Oh yes," she said reminiscing. "I talked with her nearly every day and visited her at least once a week."

"I had no idea," David said. "I didn't know you two had things in common."

"Oh yes, David," she responded. "She was my prayer partner and for the last few years I would go to her to help me understand my visions and dreams."

David jerked his head from staring at Aunt Tillie's empty chair.

"You have dreams Sister Marie?" he asked.

"Well I think everyone has dreams," Sister Marie said. "It's just that mine seem to be spiritual."

"I hope you don't mine my asking you this especially at a time like this, but - could you tell me about one?" he asked.

"Well, once I had this weird dream about people lining up to throw away something into a huge incinerator. It was really strange. They would carry the items like they were carrying sacrifices. I could never see exactly what the items were," she said sighing.

"You're the witness," David mumbled under his breath.

"What did you say?" she asked. "I said that you're my witness," David exclaimed.

Had his heart not been so heavy from the news of Aunt Tillie, he would have jumped for joy.

"Sister Marie," David asked, "did Aunt Tillie ever tell you why I came to visit her so often this year? I'm not referring to when Rose and I came to visit together."

"No, she never talked specifically about your visits," said Sister Marie. "I respected her privacy," she said.

"As it turns out," David said, "you're not the only one who needed her help with dreams. She has enfolded to me some great mysteries of God through her prayer life. For a while, I thought I was losing my mind until Aunt Tillie stepped in. It was quite a miracle, yet I know it was all in the plan of God. Last night I shared with her how I was able to pray to God for the understanding of a particular dream and God gave me the interpretation. She seemed to be so happy for me. She did say something about not feeling the best and catching a healing. I wish I had come last night like she had asked me to," he said regretfully. "She told me she had something for me. I have no idea what it was and now I may never know," he said.

"Well, I was made her trustee and power of attorney, several years ago," Sister Marie said. I'll be back to clean out this place, after funeral arrangements are made," she said sadly. "If I find anything that I think she wanted you to have, I'll be more than happy to get it to you."

"This place feels awfully empty without Aunt Tillie. Did she have any family left?" David asked.

"She's got some cousins who are rather distant. She always said our church members were her only real family. I spoke to my husband this afternoon about having a memorial service, possibly on Friday. If possible David, I'd like you to speak," she said.

David hesitated before answering Sister Marie. He took a deep breath then sighed, "I'll be happy to speak on Aunt Tillies behalf."

"Will you be alright driving home?" she asked. "You've had a terrible shock."

"I'll be fine," he said as he stood up. He looked at the flowers as if he didn't know what to do with them. Then he handed them to Sister Marie. "Would you please take these?" he asked. "I'd rather not look at them now," he said.

"I understand," Sister Marie said as she took the flowers. "Why don't you get some rest and adjust to this situation. I want you to promise me you'll call me if you need to talk," she said.

David nodded his head in agreement. He felt if he opened his mouth, tears might flow. He didn't want that; not in front of Sister Marie. They left, one behind the other in total silence.

When David arrived home, he noticed his answering machine was flashing. He wanted to ignore the message alert, but he felt obligated to listen to his calls. He pressed the button and began to undress at the same time.

"Mr. Edwards this is Darlene. I just wanted to let you know two things. My husband Keith is conscious and doing great and Mr. Edwards, it's a miracle, but we've reconciled. I'll talk to you about it soon. Have a great day." *Beep.*

"David it's Rose, if you're home please pick up the phone. OK. I'll try to reach you later. I need to tell you something, but I can't leave the message on this machine." *Beep.*

"David it's Rose calling. Please give me a call as soon as you get home. It's an emergency." *Beep.*

"David -it's Mom. I just wondered if you heard the news. Give me a call." End of messages.

David felt drained and exhausted. A few moments earlier, he had felt numb just like the day his father told him he was moving out. He really didn't feel like speaking to anyone. Instead, he went into his prayer room. He grabbed one horn of his altar and tried to give a prayer of thanksgiving. Only four words escaped his lips.

"Father I thank you." A flood of tears followed the words, making a small puddle that was absorbed by his vanilla colored carpet, but giving him a much needed release.

CHAPTER SEVENTEEN

A unt Tillies' memorial service was held the Friday morning after her death. Not more than fifty people were in attendance at the modern funeral home. Flowers were lined across the front of her steel bluish-gray casket. The benches were more comfortable than those at church, David thought. He was sure no one would want to spend very much time seated in a mortuary. The pastor gave a wonderful eulogy and then asked for David to come forth to have words. He looked at his mother for reassurance and handed his program to Stephanie to hold for him.

He slowly walked to the front and smiled at two elderly ladies that were seated on the front row. He thought to himself that they must be Aunt Tillies' cousins.

"Relationships," David began after clearing his throat, "are not always easy to establish. People drift in and out of our lives on a yearly basis. Those people who seem to cling to us, very often do us good. Some people leave us, and we never give them more than a fleeting thought. Aunt Tillie came into my life, but instead of her clinging to me, I clung to her. I discovered that I needed her more than she needed me. Her presence was comforting at a time when I needed comfort, her wisdom was incredibly sound, at a time when I needed advice. But more than any of these qualities," David said looking straight ahead to avoid the individual faces in the audience, "her relationship with God was to be envied."

"Upon visiting her on many occasions, I often would leave thinking,

I hope that I can get to know God the way Aunt Tillie knows him. In our last visits together, she prayed for me more earnestly than anyone ever could. She invested time in me and I believe it was a sound investment. She also imparted to me something that I was not aware of. She helped me to see my reason for being alive. It was a greater purpose than I could have dreamed. I do not believe that Aunt Tillie has left me after all," he said, noticing that Aunt Tillies' cousin was wiping a tear.

"She is a part of me more now than ever before. I know that Aunt Tillie never had children of her own, but I never knew my grandmother. I would kind of like to think of her as my adopted grandmother. That way she will always be a part of my family heritage. God Bless You."

Ten minutes later after a solo and the reading of Psalm 23, the service was completed. David was a bit surprised that it was over in exactly one hour. He expected others to talk about her kindness, but much to his surprise, Pastor Taylor said, "that concludes the services for the late Tillie Green. Those of you who so desire may continue with us to Redemption Cemetery."

Not quite having grasped the closure that he needed, he continued with the twenty others. He decided to ride with his mom and sister in his mom's car. Her red six cylinder Chrysler was nearly ten years old. Yet it ran almost as smoothly as the sunny day his father had drove it home.

"We have a new family car," his father said. "It almost seemed comical to think of the car as the "family car" these days.

"You did alright," Steph said as they walked together toward the parking lot. "As a matter of fact, I'm proud of you."

"Thanks Steph," David said. "How are you doing these days?"

"Pretty well," she said with a gleam in her eye. "Don't tell mom, but I'm going to have lunch with Dad on Saturday," she said, unable to contain her joy.

"Really?" David asked. "Why the secrecy?"

"He just said it was our little date. It will be just the two of us."

"That's nice," David said, imagining the conversation. He hoped that whatever they talked about would be good news.

"I am the resurrection and the life..." Pastor Taylor began "...ashes to ashes, dust to dust..."

David watched from across the rectangular grave, as Rose dropped her head in grief. He silently left the huddle of family and friends where he stood and walked behind the crowd. He ended up at Rose's side and almost without warning, offered his shoulder for her to cry on. Accepting, she wept quietly, and he never said a word.

◆

David heard laughter all around him. Nothing was that funny. But then again, the sound of the laughter was distorted and surreal. Of course, David thought. "I'm in hell."

He hid behind the shadows of tall unattractive pillars and listened as the reports were given.

"I don't know what happened. I tried to kill him. It's just that his wife kept making some strange confession about a successful marriage and she keeps reporting to that David Edwards. The plan was spoiled but I'm about to close in on David Edwards. I'll need the help of some of the others. It may be a little more complicated than I first thought because of this prayer thing he's trying. I'll put an end to that or my name isn't the Big D," he said before bursting into obnoxious laughter again.

David awoke into the darkness of the night. He had been tossing and turning for more than 30 minutes. His forehead was sweaty and his eyes struggled to adjust to the pitch blackness of his room. The only light came from the digital red clock positioned in front of him. It was only 3:30 a.m. It had been several weeks since his journey into hell.

"I'm tired of going through this," he said. He turned on his little lamp and pulled the Bible from his night stand. He shook his head and said "this is dé-jà vu". He was distracted by a light tapping at the door. He did not immediately get up because he thought it must be the wind. After the persistence of the noise he put on his robe and went to his apartment door. Looking through the peep hole he could see a distorted view of a face that reminded him of his friend Stephen. He quickly opened the door after unlocking the gold deadbolt.

"Stephen, what are you doing here?" he asked. "Are you ok?"

"Oh, I'm ok," Stephen said. "I've been driving around for the last three hours," he said, as he put what resembled a gym bag on the floor. "Myra and I had another fight. It would have looked worse if she left home at midnight, so I left. I just don't know what to do anymore David. I feel like going out and having a drink. Which is strange since I don't care for alcohol."

"Just calm down," David said yawning. "Things always appear worse in the middle of the night."

"Look I just need a place to stay for a few days, until I can figure out exactly what I'm going to do."

"Sure," David said. "You're welcome to stay with me. You must be tired after driving around for three hours. Let me get you some blankets and I think I have an extra pillow," David said.

He went into the closet of his spare room and brought down an old quilt his mom had given him when he moved. He also found a sheet, pillow and pillowcase for his friend. He felt bad that things hadn't worked out better for him. He had hoped his advice would have made a difference, but there was no time for wondering about problems. It would soon be light and there would be plenty of time to talk later. David helped Stephen get settled, sat up and talked to him a little longer and finally went to bed about 4:20 a.m.

Much to his surprise, when he awoke it was 7 a.m. He jumped up, showered, left a note and a spare key for Stephen and drove much faster than normal to work.

"I must have slept through my alarm, or had I even set it?" David questioned himself. He was turning the final corner before reaching the parking lot when he realized he hadn't prayed at all. The guilt trip would have to wait until he had settled in at work. He couldn't arrive later than his clients. He would pray in the office.

The receptionist stopped him before he could get inside his office.

"Mr. Edwards, I hope you don't mind, but I had to move a client up one slot. She has an emergency and this is the only time she had available."

David looked across the room that was half filled with people and found a rather anxious young woman smiling at him. He assumed this was the lady and told the receptionist he would see her in two minutes.

There was a full load of clients to be seen that day. New and old faces seemed to have kept the office filled. Before he knew it, the day was over. He was happy about the busyness of the day because it kept him from getting sleepy. It had been a little while since he had stayed up all night.

He returned home and noticed Stephen's car was still in front of the apartment building. He went inside and found the living area tidier than he usually kept it. There was one exception. A large black suitcase had replaced the gym bag along the far wall.

"Stephen?" David called out.

"I'm back here," Stephen yelled.

David followed the voice to his spare room and was shocked by what he found. Stephen had rearranged the room and was bending over the table that was serving as his altar. The horns had been placed beneath the table, so that Stephen's clothes and toiletries could fit neatly on the top. Stephen was bending over a gray futon which he was trying to set up against the wall. He never looked up once to see David's frowning face indicating his displeasure at the change.

"I hope you don't mind David," he explained. "This is just a temporary rearrangement in order to make sure you have the space you need. I can't tell you how it makes me feel for you to be here for me. I'll remove the suitcase from the living room, and you won't even know I'm here. I've just got to figure out what to do."

"Have you seen or spoken to Myra?" David inquired.

"No, she wasn't there when I returned to get some of my things. I think we both need time to consider our situations, but if you don't mind, I don't want to talk about it right now."

"Oh sure," David said glancing at his altar horns. He felt like he was invading Stephen's space so he went into his own bedroom. At least things there appeared untouched.

David gathered his laundry together and decided to make himself scarce for the evening. He also needed some time to think.

Once in the hallway, he heard his neighbors' door opening. He descended the stairs without waiting.

"Hey David!" yelled Michael. "How's it going? Let me know when you're having chili again," he said.

"Oh I will," said David. "How's your wife?"

"She's O.K.," he said, lowering his voice. "Say, is it expensive to attend your counseling session?"

"Not really," David said. "We offer payment plans and sometimes the fee is discounted when the family has hardships."

"Could you send me more information?" Michael asked.

"Hey, that's no problem. I'll be glad to have it mailed to you by the end of this week."

"Hey man," he said grabbing David's arm. "I'd really appreciate it."

Laundry was not a chore for David that evening. The problems he had on his mind made the time pass quickly. He hoped he had made the right decision in letting Stephen stay with him for a while. He just wished he had been asked about rearranging his prayer room. He resolved that he would use the living room to pray. It was an inconvenience, but it was better than not praying at all.

He was sure it was his Christian duty to take in Stephen. What are friends for? They would have to find a way to share the apartment space for the next few days. The dampness from the musty apartment building basement was starting to bother David's throat. He folded the clothes and left to get some throat lozenges.

He returned to the apartment with basket in hand and took the clean clothes directly into his bedroom. Stephen was not there. David went into the kitchen cupboard and found a can of chicken noodle soup. He wasn't sure how old it was, but he felt like he needed some soup. "I'm catching a healing," he said out loud. He chuckled slightly as he thought of Aunt Tillie.

After dinner he gargled with warm salt water and prepared for bed. Stephen had not returned so he thought he would turn in early. He reached for the small picture frame that held Rose's picture. It was hard for him to come to terms with what he felt. He knew he loved her. He also knew that somehow, when the time was right, God would release him to marry her. He put the picture back in its place and picked up the Bible.

His normal enthusiasm just wasn't there, and he immediately started to yawn. He blamed it on his scratchy throat, as he closed the black leather cover and fell asleep.

Laughter, heat and more laughter. That's what David was sensing as he stared into the dark. He could see no one. He extended his arms to feel for whatever was there. Yet he felt he was just groping into the darkness. Who's laughing at me? David thought. "Why am I so warm?" he said out loud. "It's hot, hot, hot!" he complained throwing the covers off him.

The alarm clock rang out loudly causing him to sit straight up. He awoke and discovered he was perspiring. Not only that, but his pajama shirt was pretty wet. He shut the alarm off and began to walk toward his prayer room out of habit. The door was shut and he remembered that he had a guest in his house. He deliberated on whether to pray in the living room, but it just didn't seem private enough. He went into the kitchen to get some water for his dry throat. He felt as though the fresh water was putting a fire out.

The fire was coming from his internal organs. He quietly went into the bathroom and got out the thermometer his mother had packed along with other basic medical supplies at the time that he was moving. Not only were his eyes red but his face looked flushed. The thermometer read 102. He hoped this was not a part of the virus that the media said had been circulating for the past three weeks. Yet, he couldn't deny filling awful. He found two aspirin in the medicine cabinet.

He wanted to pray, but instead he just crawled back into bed. He awoke again at 8 a.m. with the sound of music coming from his stereo system. He could tell he was still feverish. He opened his bedroom door and saw Stephen adjusting the volume on his system.

They looked at each other, as if neither was expecting the other one to be there. "I didn't know you were still here," Stephen said. "Hey, are you OK?"

"I've got a fever," David replied. "I feel awful. I'm going to call the Center and tell them I won't be in today."

Stephen glanced through the collection of CD's on the shelf while David called his job.

"Maybe you should call the doctor," Stephen said. "You never know why a fever develops," he warned him.

"I don't know," David said. "First I'll try these fever reducing tablets." "I hate going to see doctors. Aren't you working today?"

"I took vacation for the week to kind of help sort things out. So if you need something from the druggist, let me know," Stephen answered.

Another two hours of resting reinforced his belief that working was much more fun than being sick. He decided he must call the doctor. The number of rings was quite discouraging.

"Medical Group" a tired sounding voice finally answered.

"Hi My name is ..."

"Could you hold please?" a female voice interrupted.

David was a bit disturbed by the curtness. He was sure however, that his impatience was due to his physical condition.

"Medical Group," the voice repeated.

"This is David Edwards. I've got a 102-degree temperature and a sore throat. I wanted to know if I could see the doctor."

"Sir," the doctor is swamped today and tomorrow. Looks like every-one and his brother has some form of this latest virus. They all have rather high fevers. I recommend lots of juice and water. The best I can do is have the doctor call in an antibiotic for you. Do you know your health plan number?"

"Not off hand," David replied.

"Date of birth?" she continued.

He gave her his date of birth and was rather relieved that he didn't have to go into the office. Stephen had volunteered to pick up his medication, and he was going to take advantage of the offer.

"Sir your prescription will be available in about two hours. What pharmacy would you like to pick it up from?"

"Healthmart is just around the corner from me," David said.

The simple questions were starting to tire him out. He felt a headache developing.

"By the way," David said. "My records should show I'm allergic to certain medications."

"Thank you" she replied. "Is there anything else I can do for you today?"

'No," David answered.

He asked Stephen to pick up his medication at noon. He went back to bed. There were chills going up and down his spine. He figured the virus was attacking at full force. "I'm catching a healing," "I'm catching a healing, I'm catching a healing," he kept repeating until he had fallen asleep.

David greeted Aunt Tillie with a huge hug. "I haven't seen you in such a long time," he said.

"Are you praying," she asked. The question seemed to have reverberated over and over and over. He finally dropped his head in shame. "You're a warrior, a warrior of might. Repeat after me, I'm a warrior. I'm a warrior. I'm a warrior—."

"David! David!" shouted Stephen. "Here's your medication." David sat up in bed looking around as if he expected to see someone else.

"That must have been some dream," Stephen said. You said something about a warrior. Are you OK?"

"Well, I will be. Thanks for picking up the medicine. What time is it?" he asked.

"You've been asleep about three hours."

"What!" David exclaimed. "Seems like I just went to bed."

Stephen handed him a glass of water and his bottle of medicine. David glanced at the medication title but did not recognize the name. He then awkwardly opened it with his sweaty hands and took the capsules with hope of getting some relief.

"It says I should take another dosage in six hours. Would you wake me at nine if I'm still asleep?" David asked.

"Sure," Stephen said. "I'm going out for a while, but I should be back soon."

"See you later," David said. "I'm just tired."

It was a little while before David fell asleep. For the next thirty minutes he thought of his clients, his family, Aunt Tillie and Rose. He mostly thought of Rose. If we were married, he thought, she'd be here taking care of me. Then he felt guilty. He hadn't prayed in his prayer room. He had let someone rearrange his life temporarily. Perhaps it was just a small inconvenience or perhaps it was a plot to stop him from being a warrior. Maybe I'm paranoid, David thought. That was the last thought he had before the sharp pains hit in his abdominal area. He knew something was wrong. He wasn't imagining this kind of pain. He knew he wasn't dreaming. It hurt too bad. He decided to call the doctor's office again. That was his intention when he passed out from pain outside his bedroom as he made an attempt to reach the phone book on the kitchen counter.

CHAPTER EIGHTEEN

David would not remember the spectacular ride in the ambulance. Nor would he remember the panic of his friend Stephen trying to revive him. He had slipped into an unconscious oblivion. In the emergency room, he would be given a priority status. Virus cases and broken limbs would qualify as less important as they tried to bring him from shock and decide what had triggered such a reaction.

"What happened?" the doctor asked Stephen as the nurse and intern administered the amount of medication called out by the doctor.

"All I know," Stephen said, "is that when I left the apartment, he had taken two of these," he said showing the doctor David's medication. "He asked if I would awake him at eight so that he could take another dosage," Stephen explained.

"Who are you?" asked the doctor. "I'm his best friend. I separated from my wife a few days ago and he said I could stay with him for a while. You know, until I figured out what to do," he said.

"How long had he been taking his medication?" the doctor asked.

"I picked up the medicine for him after he called his doctor today. You don't think it was the medicine do you Doc?"

"We'll run some tests to find out. In the meantime, can you contact his closest family members?" the doctor asked.

"Sure, I'll call his mom." Stephen said. "Is he going to be alright?" he asked.

"He seems to have had a classic allergic reaction to this particular drug. It sends your body into shock. I'm sorry I can't discuss it any further without family."

"I'll call her right now," Stephen said.

There was no easy way to tell this parent that her child was in serious trouble. Yet, Stephen did the best he could to cause her not to panic.

Faye Edwards took the news better than Stephen imagined. She said she would call her husband and have him meet her there. When she called the office of Dennis Edwards, her brave act had been reduced to a whisper.

"Dennis," she said. "Meet me at the hospital. David is gravely ill."

"Who is this?" her husband asked after trying to recognize the voice.

"It's Faye," she snapped. "David is unconscious."

"What happened?" he asked, trying to gather his thoughts which were racing at an uncontrollable speed.

"I don't know," she answered.

"Are you home?" he asked. She nodded.

"Are you home, Faye?" he asked again.

"Yes, yes I'm home," she said.

"I'll be there to pick you up as quickly as possible," he said. "Try to stay calm."

They said very few words on the way to the hospital. Mostly because they were afraid to talk. She did tell him that Stephanie was at an all-day field trip and wouldn't be home before six that evening. They both agreed it was best not to upset her so far away from home.

The hospital receptionist informed them that David was on the third floor. Faye Edwards walked faster than normal to keep up with the pace of her husband. When they got to Room 307, they paused briefly, looked at one another and took a deep breath before opening the door.

The sound of a beeping machine and a nurse recording data from a printout nearly went unnoticed by Faye Edwards. She immediately went to the bedside of her son who appeared to be sleeping and called his name. When he didn't answer, she grabbed his hand, ignored the intravenous tubing and started to cry.

The nurse looked at them both and said she would be right back with the doctor.

"I guess she didn't want to answer any of our questions," Dennis Edwards said.

The door opened slowly and a well-groomed woman that could have been 50 years old appeared ahead of the nurse. Her hair was pulled back and tied with a silky scarf, while a stethoscope adorned her neck.

"Hi, I'm Doctor Payne," she said, extending her hand.

"I'm Dennis Edwards and this is Faye Edwards. We're David's parents."

"What happened?" they both asked at the same time.

She smiled and looked at them both in a very caring way. "I know you both have lots of questions, so I'll explain to you what we know at this time," she said.

"Your son was feverish and called his doctor for a prescription. When he got the prescription he took two pills, according to his friend Stephen who was with him at the time. The medication he took had derivatives of penicillin in it."

"Penicillin!" Faye Edwards blurted. "He's highly allergic to that," she said staring at her husband.

"That's right," Dr. Payne continued. "A short time later his body went into shock and what we call a low grade coma." "We're basically trying to give him a drug that counters the affect that the penicillin has had on him." In most cases, the drug has been very successful. Yet sometimes, I'll be totally honest with you, sometimes the patient is nonresponsive to the drug.

His vital signs are good and the drug usually works after about eight hours. It's been two hours," she said.

"Is it true that comatose patients can hear what's being said?" Faye Edwards asked.

"We do have some medical proof that in certain cases, the hearing is unaffected by the coma. For those reasons, we do encourage caution in discussing the medical condition while in the presence of the patient. Upon arrival we did a cat scan and brain waves are normal. Let's keep our fingers crossed or pray if you so desire."

"Thank you, Doctor," Dennis Edwards said.

"By the way, David's friend Stephen is in the family waiting room. He might be able to give you some more information on exactly what took place. I'll be back in a few hours to check his vitals. If you need me, any of the nurses can page me," she said, before leaving the room.

The hospital is a world of its own. Time passes but no one notices. Everyone is preoccupied with thoughts of what might have been done, what ought to be done and why haven't they tried this.

Stephen offered all the support he could. He felt awkward admitting that he and his wife were estranged. He was glad that they didn't probe further regarding his separation. He offered to go back to the apartment and check the messages for David in addition to calling his job. Secretly, he also planned to call Myra. Somehow, David's situation had jarred him into thinking that life was short. He didn't want to live it with regrets. He also thought it would be best for David's parents to wait the situation out without interruptions from the outside.

Eight hours after having received the medication for countering the penicillin, there was no change in David's condition.

"I'm going to call the Pastor," Faye announced to her husband. "I meant to do it earlier but I got distracted."

"That's a good idea," her husband said. "I'll have Doctor Payne paged, we need to find out what's going on."

Dr. Payne met with them in the family waiting room. No one else was there. "We have no explanation to why he is still comatose," the doctor said, showing a bit of nervousness that was not seen earlier. "There are other drugs to try, but we run the risk of triggering another reaction at this stage. I'm afraid we are sort of stuck in a wait and see mode. I'll let you know if there's any change. I'll be in the area if I'm needed," she said before leaving. She walked out the door and a familiar face walked in.

"Sister Marie!" Faye Edwards said with excitement as she hugged her tightly around the neck.

"Thank you so much for coming!"

"What do you mean?" Sister Marie said. "He's my son too, I adopted him when he wasn't looking. The Pastor was speaking to one of the nurses, he'll join us in a moment," Sister Marie said. I understand an allergic reaction caused this," she said.

"That's right," Faye Edwards interjected. "Somebody wasn't doing their job and gave my baby penicillin," she said, getting very emotional.

"Don't upset yourself any more than you already have Faye," Dennis Edwards said.

"I'm trying to be calm," she said. "It's just not fair. He's such a good boy."

"Don't you think the Lord knows that Faye?" Sister Marie said comfortingly.

"Now our job is to pray and believe God that this nightmare will be over soon." At that instant, Pastor Taylor entered. He shook hands with Dennis Edwards and hugged Faye.

"You know that Marie and I are here for you, don't you?" he asked. "I've already instructed Rose to get the prayer chain started."

"How is she taking it?" Faye Edwards asked.

"She's in the room with him now. But she drove her own car because she thought she might stay late."

"She's a sweet girl," Faye Edwards said, not much louder than a whisper.

"Well, I'm just going to hang out in this sitting room for a little while. I can't stand just watching him. He looks so - so lifeless," Faye continued.

"I wish you wouldn't use those words," her husband said with a grim look. "That's rather depressing."

"I'm sorry," she said sarcastically. "I'll try to brush up on my word choices. I wouldn't want to upset you with a bad choice of words."

"Situations of this sort can be pretty intense and cause a lot of family strain," Pastor Taylor said jumping in, hoping to prevent a fight. "Why don't I say a prayer regarding God's will," he continued in his pastoral mode.

"Oh, it's God's will that my son be healed alright," said Dennis Edwards rather forcefully. "I won't pray anything to the contrary."

Just as he stood up to make his point, Rose came through the door. Following her was a couple holding hands. Rose embraced Faye Edwards and Dennis Edwards and managed a little smile. Her face was streaked with black lines and her eyes were slightly puffy. Everyone knew she had been crying. I wanted you to meet this couple. David's job told this lady what happened when she called to schedule her last appointment with him.

"Hi, I'm Darlene. This is my husband Keith," she said pointing to a man with a long facial scar who was using a crutch. We heard about David's illness and felt like we had to come down here," she said. "Otherwise people might never know," she said smiling.

"Know what?" Faye asked with a puzzled look on her face. "Keith, honey, why don't you sit down," Darlene said, pulling a chair closer for her husband.

"David helped to save our marriage," she said grabbing Keith's cane and kneeling at his chair. "I went to see him recently for counseling. I was depressed, and had lost weight and was having problems on my job. He seemed to not only counsel me, but I felt like I was a personal case. As if he were a one man crusade sent from God to save me. I tried to resist at first, but I couldn't help it," she said looking directly at Dennis Edwards. "He was determined to get me back on track."

"And of course I had no idea any of this was happening," Keith said. "I was feeling like a failure and blaming myself for past mistakes, while at the same time making a mess of my life."

"Although David is young, he seemed to have wisdom beyond his years," Darlene continued. "He taught me one thing that I didn't understand. Prayer is not a tool to be taken for granted. I was so hurt that I wasn't really praying. I was more or less just complaining to God. David taught me about confession and facing my problem. Then I began to sincerely pray for my husband in spite of the hurt that I felt," she said looking at her husband.

"Then a few weeks ago, I was in a terrible accident," Keith said. "It was one of the best things that ever happened to me. I experienced God in a way that I had not known before. In the time that I recuperated, I learned the basics about being a husband and father. I can't begin to tell you how my eyes have come opened. I shudder when I think that this could have been the end of the Smith family," he said shaking his head.

"Smith, did you say, what did you say your names were again?" asked Pastor Taylor.

"Keith and Darlene Smith," Keith answered.

"My God, I don't believe it," Pastor Taylor said, getting up quickly from his chair. "This is incredible."

"What's incredible?" asked Sister Marie.

"The fact that,"

"Excuse me," said a young man followed by a woman as he opened the door to the family waiting room. "I'm looking for the family of David Edwards."

"I'm his mother," Faye said, speaking before anyone else.

"I'm Dennis Edwards, David's father."

"Hi, I'm David's neighbor Michael. This is my wife Brenda. We just learned of what happened to David when we got in from work. I just wanted to come and give support after all that he's done for me and Brenda," he said.

"What do you mean?" asked Faye.

"Well we've only lived next door to him a short time, but he had us over for chili one night and planted some life changing seeds into my life. I never really got a chance to tell him what a difference it made for the way I was living and trying to survive in my marriage," Michael said.

"I'm not ashamed to say I saw a difference right away," Brenda said. "I was impressed by the things Michael started doing differently. It's all so strange, even the way we ended up living there. I really believe it was God's plan."

"Let me tell you both something you don't know," Pastor Taylor said. "David was assigned to pray for you both before he met you. He told me so. I know it sounds incredible because I didn't believe it either. He called off his plans to marry my daughter Rose, because he had a divine assignment to help you. Rose, I know I never told you this because I thought David just had marriage jitters. He said he couldn't marry you until God gave him permission. It had nothing to do with his love for you. I repent before God and all of you for being blind to what he was trying to tell me," Pastor Taylor said, pulling out a handkerchief.

Rose got up from her seat and hugged her father. She wept and he hugged her ever so gently.

The McCain's and the Smith's said their goodbyes and promised to keep David in their prayers and believe God for a miracle.

"I think I'll go back and sit in his room for a while," Rose said.

The room seemed so full of love with everyone there telling their stories. When the five left, a silence fell over the group.

"We still haven't had that prayer," Pastor Taylor said. "Let's hold..."

The door opened again and when they looked up there were two young ladies there. No one knew what to think.

"Hi Sister Marie," one of the young ladies said warmly.

"Clarissa? DeBorah? Hi! How are you? Who are you ladies here visiting?"

"We heard about Brother David Edwards through the prayer chain," DeBorah said.

"Well that's nice of you to come out here to see him," Sister Marie said.

"Not really," said Clarissa. "Are you David's parents?" she asked looking at Dennis and Faye Edwards."

"Yes, we are." said Dennis Edwards.

"I just want you to know that David along with Sister Marie helped to save my life," Clarissa said. "Mine too!" said DeBorah.

"I didn't think you two even knew each other before our women's meeting," said Sister Marie.

"Actually we didn't," said DeBorah. We were both referred to the counseling service by different people. I saw Clarissa several times as I was coming and going from the center. Then as strange as it sounds, we were the only single ladies invited to your group," DeBorah said.

"After that, we started talking to one another and discovered that we had a lot in common. We were both dealing with low self-esteem problems and we both were well, suicidal. After we talked, we found out why we didn't like ourselves, thanks to David. He told us certain things in common. We were the fruit of the womb, created by God. To kill ourselves would be to destroy the very fruit that God had intended for a purpose. The more he talked, the more I understood that I had been listening to the lies of the Devil. We might be bruised, but we are still fruit and thanks to David we plan to have fruitful lives. The very fact that Sister Marie invited us to that luncheon, confirmed that we were important to God," DeBorah said.

"We're not going to take up your time, we just wanted to see David and let you know we are praying for him," Clarissa said.

Sister Marie went forward and hugged them both. Faye followed and they left.

"Something is happening here for a reason," Pastor Taylor said.

"Dennis, did you realize the impact your son was having on other people's lives?" the pastor asked.

Dennis Edwards was all choked up. He did his best to keep his composure. "Pastor, can we pray now?" he asked, in a very humble but direct way. "If you don't mind, I'd like to lead the prayer."

Dennis Edwards grabbed the hand of his wife and held it tightly. Sister Marie and Pastor Taylor completed the circle.

"Dear God," Dennis Edwards began, "forgive me for my selfishness and my pride and for what I did to my family. He took one of his hands and wiped the tears that began to flow like a fountain. "I'm sorry God," he said wiping his nose with the handkerchief that Pastor Taylor placed in his hand, "for hurting my, my- wife and kids." At that point he threw his arms around Faye and they both wept together.

Sister Marie took her husband by the hand and nearly pulled him from the room. "Let's give them some privacy," she said. "They've got a lot of hurt to be healed and they don't need us to witness the process. Let's go check on David," she said.

On the way down the hall they nearly ran head on into Stephanie.

"What's wrong with my brother?" she said in a hysterical tone. "Where's my mother and father? Please tell me something."

"Are you just finding out?" Sister Marie asked with amazement.

"I've been on an all-day field trip. When I got home people kept calling and asking about David."

"Have you seen him?" Pastor Taylor asked.

"Yes, sir," but no one was around to tell me what's wrong with him," she said, trying to catch her breath.

"I guess Rose must have stepped out," Sister Marie said. "David had an allergic reaction to some medication he was taking. Right now he's in a coma." Stephanie clasped her hand over her mouth to keep from giving the loud outburst that she felt in her stomach.

"Stephanie you're going to calm yourself and go to his bedside. He needs to hear your voice," Sis. Marie said.

"Now Marie don't disillusion the child," Pastor Taylor said.

"Honey, I'm not just saying that, I feel that within my spirit."

On the way to the room Rose met them as she left the ladies room. She gave Stephanie a hug and held on to her.

They walked in the room and Steph took the seat closest to David. The others stood back at the foot of the bed. Stephanie took his hand and looked at Sister Marie. The nod that Sister Marie gave must have been all the reassurance that she needed to talk with her brother. She stroked his hand and told him stories of childhood memories. He was always there to help her and get her out of trouble. She reminded him that he said he would take her to the prom to keep all the guys away. Then she laughed and told him he had better wake up because someone else had asked her today if she had a date. She closed her eyes for a moment, when she felt a tug. She thought perhaps a jerk reaction was taking place while she stroked his hand. When she opened her eyes, she saw that David had actually gripped her hand loosely and was holding it.

"Hallelujah," Sister Marie said with tears of joy coming down her face. "Did you see that? Rose get the doctor. Honey, get Faye and Dennis, look - David is starting to wake up!" she said with enough excitement to scare everyone into action.

Chapter Nineteen

D r. Payne didn't really want to, but she found it necessary to put everyone out of the room while she assessed David's condition. To describe their exuberance as joyful would be an understatement.

While David's eyes were still unresponsive, both his hands were moving and he was starting to breathe faster. The signs were all good according to the doctor. While he had been comatose for thirteen hours, she said she was surprised at the body movements and was sure he would gain consciousness at any time.

Stephanie nearly fainted when her father came down the hall with his arm around her mother. She had to sit down because she thought she was dreaming. But she wasn't. She wanted to cry but she couldn't. Her emotions had all run away. Inside she was thrilled, but one side of her said it was only a dream. She couldn't get up from the hall chair. She sat there until they came to her and lifted her into the circle of their world. One big hug. It felt so good. She thought she would melt.

Thirty minutes later, Dr. Payne asked for the immediate family to join her in the room. They walked in and found David was looking up at them. His mother kissed him and his father kissed him too. Afterwards, his parents kissed each other. David looked confused. Then he smiled.

"Mom," he said.

"David don't try to say too much, you've been through quite an ordeal," Dr. Payne said.

"But I've got to tell you where I've been," he said. "I was in a dark place and I was trying to find my way home. I could hear the demons rejoicing. They thought their plot had worked. Then they got angry because it was falling apart. Can I have some water?" he asked.

His mother quickly poured him some water and helped him sit up to take a few sips.

"The demons started coming after me. The demons kept telling Big D to get me. I found out that was Disease. They wanted to give me a disease. I kept running. Then I heard Aunt Tillie's voice. She kept saying, 'prayer warriors are always one step ahead of the devil.' Whenever it seemed like they were getting close, I would hear her saying, 'the blood of Jesus covers you David.' It would give me more confidence to keep going. I just wanted to go home. Then finally I heard Stephanie's voice. It was so real. She was singing that same song I heard her sing before. Then I understood this time what it meant.

I guess I never told you about her song, the words are "From generation to generation thou hast been our dwelling place." David paused for a moment because he was out of breath. Then he started talking again. "Will you now restore us with your mercy and your grace. Lord break we now all images that don't reflect your love. We turn from selfish pleasures and seek thy face above. All of a sudden," he said, "I woke up."

"See, King Josiah repented for his people and for the ways of his ancestors that had strayed from God. The books of the law had been lost for so long because little by little the ways of God were forgotten. After King Josiah repented on behalf of everyone, he brought out the books and they listened to the words of the Lord all day long. It was like a beautiful song. And that's what Stephanie's song is - we've found the words of the Lord again."

"That's beautiful son," Dennis Edwards said. "I want you to know that your mother and I have found the book that was lost in the temple. I decided I don't want a counterfeit, I want the real thing. Thanks for leading me back to the light," he said placing a hand on Faye's shoulder.

"Is Rose here?" David asked.

She's right outside," his mother said. "We'll leave while you talk with her," she said. One by one they filed out the room and Rose was summoned to come inside.

Rose came into the room and sat at his side. "How are you feeling?" she said feeling awkward but happy. He took her hand and placed it in his.

"Rose, I - I know I hurt you in the past. I'm truly sorry for that. I didn't know how to handle what I was going through."

"I wish you would have trusted me," she said. "I'm sorry you went through so much alone," she continued.

"Well, I wasn't totally alone. I had Aunt Tillie. I don't know what I would have done without her. As soon as the current situations are over, I can resume my life, our life," he said.

"What situations?" she asked.

"Well there are some people that- wait a minute," he said. "I can cross one couple off my list."

"You can cross three couples off your list," she said. "Keith and Darlene have reconciled and so have your neighbors Michael and Brenda McCain." she said with pleasure.

"How did you know about them?" he asked.

"They came to visit you and told us how you had helped them."

"Then who's the third couple Rose? Are you talking about me and you?" he asked.

"No, I'm talking about your mom and dad. I know you've been praying for them too."

"How did?-" David began.

"I understand a lot more than you give me credit for," she said. "I went to help my stepmom clean out Aunt Tillie's apartment. I didn't tell her but I found a Bible that Aunt Tillie had left for you." She pulled from her purse a small Bible covered with beautiful black leather that was well worn but in great shape. She pulled open the cover and read an inscription.

"My dearest David, just like your name, you're a mighty prayer warrior, a natural leader and seeking after the heart of God. May this small gift remind you always to seek the face of God, love his people and never be intimidated by any demon in hell. A prayer warrior is always one step ahead of the devil. Love Always, Aunt Tillie."

David took the Bible and rubbed his hand gently across the leather. "Rose," he asked, looking up directly into her face, "Will you marry me?"

Chapter Twenty

David was sure that the church could not have seen a more beautiful bride. A thousand thoughts ran through his mind as he watched her glowing like the eastern star as she came closer and closer to the front. He smiled at Stephen, who stood behind him as his best man. Stephen acknowledged the smile by nodding his head approvingly. Then he looked into the audience and smiled at Myra. Stephen couldn't begin to explain his feelings of thankfulness.

David felt as secure as a babe in the womb. He had his family in the same room at the same time, witnessing the most special day of his life. The pain of the last few years seemed only a vague memory. What was real was in front of him. His parents were seated together in church. He knew they weren't perfect but he saw two individuals put aside their selfish desires in order for the will of God to go forth. Yet, to David, that was as perfect as any marriage could get.

The outcome of each situation was worth every trip he had made into hell.

The audience stood and stared in awe as the beautiful bride marched with timely rhythm to the traditional wedding march. She clung to her father with her gloved hand but stared at the awaiting groom.

The two eagerly approached the altar after her father released her. He nodded approvingly as he gave her to the one who would be responsible for her from that day forward.

David had insisted on writing his own vows. He said he had things to acknowledge to the Lord. He was not afraid to speak vows before God and man. He knew God would enable him to keep those vows.

"I, David Jonathan Edwards, promise before God and all these witnesses to love you Rose Marie as Christ loved the church. I know that I have a lot of growing to do in order to achieve that promise. I know that I may never love you the exact way that Christ does, but I vow to spend the rest of my life trying. As you have been presented to me today, a beautiful woman, I present myself to you though I know I am not flawless. As you look to me for protection, I will look to Christ, as you look to me for provision, I will look to Christ, as you look to me for understanding, I will look to Christ and if you should ever look to me for forgiveness, I will look to Christ. Christ has become my model. I will look to him daily in order to view my image in his mirror. As time goes by, should God grant us any precious seed, I promise to nurture the seed in the ways of the Lord without sacrificing my promises to you to fulfill your needs. These are the promises I make to God first, to you second and finally before the witnesses of this assembly, so help me God."

Rose fought back the tears as she held his hand. Somehow she knew in her heart that not one of these words would fall to the ground. They were being permanently branded in his heart as well as hers and she would never forget them.

◆

One week after the wedding, the chase was on. David dreamed demons were running all over the place. He overheard an argument that had developed between Satan and the demons.

As it turns out, neither the Smiths nor the McCains were the real target. Satan announced that he was really after the children, the seed of man, the fruit of God. Yet, since his demons failed to get the parents, he would have a terrible time getting to the children. There was no one in line to be sacrificed. At least no one that David knew. Yet every direction he turned, he could hear the demons taking flight. They were actually running and confused.

He woke up and grinned. For the first time in his dream, he was the aggressor. The enemy was actually running from him. They were afraid of the power he exercised through prayer.

No one was beside him. Where was Rose? The clock showed five a.m. She was probably in the bathroom, he reasoned. As he entered his prayer room he was pleasantly surprised to find her there. She had one hand on the horn of the altar. Then she looked up, gave him a smile and extended the other hand to her husband.

The End

About the Author

Sandra Thompson Williams is a native of Saint Louis, Missouri. Raised in a Christian home, she received her bachelor's degree in Communication from St. Louis University and worked more than 15 years in public relations for educational institutions. She also worked in several capacities for St. Louis County Library.

In addition to "Eating the Fruit of Lies," she has written two other novels, "The Invocation," and "The Last Three Tickets to Heaven." She has also authored a devotional, "Even Better than Aunt Harvey's Greens," and co-wrote a biography titled, "Ye Shall Receive Power: The Spiritual Life of Vera Boykin." She also has a Bible study publication titled, "Seven Miracles of Prevailing Praise."

A praise and worship leader at her local church, Sandra enjoys the music that reaches the heart of the Father. In 2012, she released her first CD titled Songs of Deliverance.

A licensed missionary through her local assembly, she is also a dedicated Sunday School teacher.

In addition to writing, Sandra enjoys singing, traveling and discovering hidden truths in the Bible. She resides in the St. Louis metropolitan area.